NEW YORK REVIEW BOOKS
CLASSICS

T0021041

MARGERY KEMPE

ROBERT GLÜCK (b. 1947) is the author of two novels, *Margery Kempe* and *Jack the Modernist*; two short-story collections, *Elements* and *Denny Smith*; *Communal Nude: Collected Essays*; and, most recently, *About Ed* (published by New York Review Books). His books of poetry include *Reader*, *La Fontaine* with Bruce Boone, and *In Commemoration of the Visit* with Kathleen Fraser. He made an artist book, *Parables*, with Jose Angel Toirac and Meira Marrero Díaz, and he wrote the preface to *Between Life and Death*, a book of paintings by Frank Moore. With Camille Roy, Mary Burger, and Gail Scott, he edited the anthology *Biting the Error: Writers Explore Narrative*. In the late 1970s, Glück and Bruce Boone founded New Narrative, a literary movement that makes use of self-reflexive storytelling and essay, lyric, and autobiography in one work. Glück served as the director of the Poetry Center at San Francisco State University, where he is an emeritus professor. He was the co-director of Small Press Traffic Literary Center and an associate editor at Lapis Press. He lives "high on a hill" in San Francisco.

COLM TÓIBÍN is the author of nine novels, including *The Master* and *Brooklyn*, and two collections of stories. His play *The Testament of Mary* was nominated for a Tony Award for Best Play in 2013. He is the Mellon Professor of the Humanities at Columbia University.

MARGERY KEMPE

ROBERT GLÜCK

Introduction by
COLM TÓIBÍN

NEW YORK REVIEW BOOKS

New York

THIS IS A NEW YORK REVIEW BOOK
PUBLISHED BY THE NEW YORK REVIEW OF BOOKS
207 East 32nd Street, New York, NY 10016
www.nyrb.com

"My Margery, Margery's Bob" originally appeared in *Shark*, no. 3, fall 2000, and was collected in *Communal Nude: Collected Essays* by Robert Glück, published in 2016 by Semiotext(e).

Library of Congress Cataloging-in-Publication Data
Names: Glück, Robert, 1947– author. | Tóibín, Colm, 1955– writer of
  introduction.
Title: Margery Kempe / by Robert Gluck, introduction by Colm Toibin.
Description: New York : New York Review Books, [2020] | Series: New York
  review books classics | Copyright © 1994 by Robert Gluck, introduction
  copyright © 2020 by Colm Toibin.
Identifiers: LCCN 2019039532 (print) | LCCN 2019039533 (ebook) | ISBN
  9781681374314 (paperback) | ISBN 9781681374321 (ebook)
Subjects: LCSH: Kempe, Margery, approximately 1373– —Fiction. | Women
  mystics—Fiction. | Gay men—Fiction. | GSAFD: Love stories.
Classification: LCC PS3557.L82 M37 2020 (print) | LCC PS3557.L82 (ebook) |
  DDC 813/.54—dc23
LC record available at https://lccn.loc.gov/2019039532
LC ebook record available at https://lccn.loc.gov/2019039533

ISBN 978-1-68137-431-4
Available as an electronic book; ISBN 978-1-68137-432-1

Printed in the United States of America on acid-free paper.
10 9 8 7 6 5 4 3 2

CONTENTS

INTRODUCTION

Some way into *Margery Kempe*, Robert Glück ends a chapter with a question: "How can the two halves of this novel ever be closed or complete? Or the book is a triptych: I follow L. on the left, Margery follows Jesus on the right, and in the center my fear hollows out 'an empty space that I can't fill.'" It is characteristic of this free-wheeling, intriguing, and self-aware novel to shift tone and change direction so abruptly. The two halves of the novel referred to are, on the one hand, the story of the narrator's love affair with a handsome, evasive, and elusive American aristocrat, the so-called L., and, on the other hand, the story of Margery Kempe, an English Christian mystic, born around 1473, who wrote what is often called the first autobiography in English.

The centerpiece of the triptych, rather than an empty space, is actually a daring literary style that favors startling images that move from late fourteen- and early fifteenth-century England to late twentieth-century America with suddenness and ingenuity. The sentences have a way of holding their nerve, like someone driving on ice braking hard on a sharp turn. The book plays not only with time but with tone. It allows moments or emotions from one story to leak into the other, in the same way as one thought in consciousness loses its sway and lets something more immediate take its place, only to be supplanted in turn by another thought or image. What connects the stories and weaves its way through the book is the theme of death, death that comes from hopeless infatuation, from sexual desire, from plagues new and old.

Nothing is schematic in *Margery Kempe*. Its procedures, connecting the deeply personal with the experimental, are underpinned by a theory of fiction-writing called New Narrative that was proposed by Robert Glück and some associates in San Francisco in the 1970s.

The competing narratives in *Margery Kempe* work against expectations; they obey no rules. The novel allows the stories and voices to wander, as the mind might wander, following arrangements that are more organic than orderly. The book does not accept the idea of story itself as a single line and does not have sections that are intact, contained, discrete. It seeks to undermine the very notion of the master narrative, or even competing narratives, to be replaced by a sort of porousness or flow.

"My palette is a sentence. Each next sentence can start at a very different place and so that makes for a kind of porousness, which is a quality I want," Glück said in an interview with *EOAGH*, in the spring of 2009. There are sentences in the book that seem to establish verisimilitude, but then the sentences coming next appear to parody that very possibility. There are moments that set up a time and a place to be followed by language that is deliberately out-of-date.

In the same interview, Glück said: "In *Margery*, for instance, all the birds are real, even in her visions of the Holy Land, the right birds appear where and when they should. All the clothing is accurate. Other things are purposely anachronistic."

While the novel thus undermines stable ideas of time, it is held together by a delight in what phrases and sentences do, by a rhythmic vivacity in the texture of the prose that compels the attention, enters the nervous system almost stealthily until the structures that the book sets out to question, having been purified by holy fire, return to us, ready to be taken seriously.

The novel is filled with images of the body, of pure carnality and quick desire. In their introduction to the anthology *Writers Who Love Too Much: New Narrative 1977–1997*, Kevin Killian and Dodie Bellamy wrote: "Before there was crowd-sourcing, Bob [Glück] was asking his friends and students to provide lists of body sensations that he subsequently sifted into his novel on Margery Kempe." The novel allows religious devotion itself to soar above the mere business of prayer and obedience into a realm that is filled with the possibilities of bliss and fulfillment, not only for the soul but for the body, the body that holds the center of each side panel of the triptych.

The figure of Jesus in the novel is brought to earth. He is all sex and sinew. Margery's devotion is not to the word Jesus preached or the promise of heaven, it is to his flesh, the living reality of his presence on earth, his mundane existence. His lubricity, rather than his preaching, is his allure.

"The tension between masculine-feminine and inside-outside pervades all levels of my community," the narrator writes. On the same page, it is as though the narrator's desire for L. and Margery's for Jesus become interwoven, just as, soon afterward, words like "man," "woman," "me," "I," "he" start to become interpenetrative. Soon the sexual desire in the novel becomes a single one, or one in which all boundaries have been threatened. "I push myself under the surface of Margery's story, holding my breath for a happy ending to my own."

If this is intense, then its earnestness will not be allowed to dominate. It will soon be thwarted by Jesus saying to

Margery that he would like to send her "to Jerusalem and to Rome" and Margery replying: "Jesus, where will I get the money?" For any reader, "Jesus" here will have two meanings: one to denote the figure in the New Testament, the other a casual word often placed at the beginning of a sentence to express wonder, worry, or surprise. No matter what, the tone has shifted. If the reader's expectations are simple, they will have been wrong-footed. The narrative will have claimed a small victory over easy expectation and gained energy accordingly.

In Part Two of the book, Margery, complete with her visions and free of all fear, sets out with a group on a pilgrimage. She speaks her mind and that alarms her fellow pilgrims. The writing about nature and travel comes to us ambiguously, many declarative sentences denoting the look or feel of things as in an ordinary novel, but each of them having an edge of pastiche, put there for show, as though cut and pasted from an imagined kitty of earlier sources to make sure we take nothing for granted.

Here we have an early fifteenth century swirling with images of sex and gender, and then this pastoral landscape disrupted by contemporary concerns, as in: "Women carded and combed, clouted and washed, and peeled rushes.... One woman became a man when he jumped over an irrigation ditch and his cunt dropped inside out: gender is the extent we go to in order to be loved. His mittens were made of rags."

That last sentence may seem unnecessary, or just tagged on, but it is not. First of all, after the previous assertion, which requires us to stop for a moment, the sentence about the mittens seems natural, encouraging us to read on. It is the sort of odd detail that fiction thrives on, appearing to be part of the random visible world rather than the writer's efforts to manage reality and create schemes. Also, the sentence has a rhythm and a sound that could be from a ballad.

When stray sentences in the novel, such as "They talked till stars appeared above the elms," have a full iambic pentameter sound, it is as though they have earned their keep against the surrounding mixture of the dead serious, the parodic, the flippant, the urgent, and the real. As in "His mittens were made of rags," they have a way of restoring the possibility of innocence to a simple statement in sonorous prose. In *Communal Nude: Collected Essays*, Glück wrote: "In my novel *Margery Kempe* ... each sentence is a kind of promise, an increment of hope that replaces the broken promise of the last sentence. What is that promise? That the world will continue, that one image will replace the next forever—that is, the world will respond to your love by loving you back. The silence is that of a world about to be born."

Just as Margery goes to Venice, so too do our twentieth-century lovers. When Glück writes "Venice grew crowded as spring progressed. At dusk the population spilled into the streets and piazzas, sweetly murmurous, still dazed from the light," it is playfully clear that this is what both Margery and the lovers experienced. They have been captured in time. In *Communal Nude*, Glück wrote: "History is endlessly porous; so instead of creating a middle distance, I used extreme close-ups, historical long shots, and autobiography."

They have also been captured in prose, brought into our presence courtesy of style. There are times when the couplings between the narrator and L. require a style that is lofty, distant, made up of disparate moments, creating images of lovers who are singularly unclose. Margery and Jesus, on the other hand, experience a coupling that is more passionate and open and demands the unembarrassed style of romance writing: "She lay facing him, her red hair fanned out behind. Arms and legs draped over each other, lips touched in ardent peace."

There are moments in the book that are designed to give

us a spectacular shock. These mostly center on the figure of Jesus. Glück is unafraid of offering him a full humanity and a frailer divinity. It is noted early in the book that "He had been crying all weekend." Later, he states, "I spasmed eleven times." Later again, "Jesus and Mary squatted, making little cries, then looked curiously at each other's shit." This is no more blasphemous than Renaissance paintings showing Jesus's bare legs and thighs, his naked torso, his face in ecstasy and agony. He has always been there for us, flesh and blood.

Such waverings in the book from the sacred to the profane mirror Glück's own movements as an author. He seeks both to control the tone and follow the aleatory flow of his own inspiration. He wishes to tell both Margery's story in all its fervid strangeness and his own in all its calm melancholy. He wishes to invoke the shock and pain of the Crucifixion in a time when gay men were dying of AIDS. But he also wishes to intercede on behalf of the narrator as intruder, interloper, the man who wrote the book and will have to live outside its pages into the future: "I am drawn to modernism but my faith is impure. I am no more the solitary author of this book than I alone invent the fiction of my life. As I write, I read my experience as well as Margery's. Is that appropriation?—that I am also the reader, oscillating in a nowhere between what I invent and what changes me?"

Margery comes back to England. Dates are given, as elsewhere in the book, to establish verisimilitude. For Glück, this is a loaded idea, one he seeks both to explore and explode. It matters that the reader believes that the difficult truth and moments of pain he experiences with L., his lover, are true, or as true as he can make them, and as revealing as Margery was in her writing when she sought to reveal the quality of her devotion and vision.

Our narrator has visions too: "I raise my eyes to a dark window seven stories high where L. lives in New York. The window is lit, he is flesh and blood, he leans into another man in amusement and then warmth. I whisper his name to elevate this story with the strength of my sexuality."

In chapter 41, it is as though two mystical unions have become one, as Jesus almost becomes L., as the prose moves into italics and stray phrases. In *Communal Nude*, Glück wrote: "I draw together the emergence of the modern self and the end of the modern self, the decaying society in which Kempe lived, the decaying society in which I live, and our respective plagues. L.'s ruling-class status equals the divinity of Jesus.... The two stories are like transparencies; each can be read only in terms of the other."

Three chapters later, we read: "It was 1420; experience was crumbling." In Glück's world, the crumbling of experience is part of the deal, including the experience of reading. In the interview in *EOAGH*, he said: "The best reading is an uncertain reading.... We are educated to think that we should be able to know the meaning of a piece of writing, but what if the intention of the writing is to throw us into confusion, induce a state of wonder, and unravel the basic tenets of our experience?"

The rest then, for everyone involved, is a plot that cannot be given away. It is all the more precious because it has been foretold, and its telling includes cries and whispers as well as questions: "How do you find your way in empty desert when you have become that desert?"

—Colm Tóibín

MARGERY KEMPE

ACKNOWLEDGMENTS

For the most part I used B. A. Windeatt's transla-
tion, *The Book of Margery Kempe*, phrases of which remain
undigested in my book. I relied on Louise Collis's
Memoirs of a Medieval Woman, along with other sources,
such as *Three Prose Works* by John Aubrey, the notebooks
of the eighteenth-century naturalist Gilbert White, and
miniatures from books of hours. I found the epigraph for
Margery in Michael Baxandall's *Painting and Experience in
Fifteenth Century Italy*.

As I say in chapter thirty, I gathered observations
and anecdotes about the body and dropped them into my
shadowy fifteenth-century characters. I wanted to mingle
the near and distant, present a jumpy, heterogeneous
physical life, and assert the present, which projects in
every direction. I owe a debt of gratitude to the following friends who gave me their observations in the form
of notes: Steve Abbott, Honor Johnson, Sarah Schulman,
Thom Gunn, Fanny Howe, Lyn Hejinian, Robin Trem-
bley McGraw, Susan King, Bonnie Kernes, Rachel
Barkley, Jane Longaway, Matias Viegener, Gina Hyams,
Lisa Bernstein, Bo Huston, Frances Jaffer, Carla

Harryman, Kevin Killian, Dodie Bellamy, Warren Sonbert, Elin Elisofon, Camille Roy, Bruce Boone, Michael Amnasan, and Frances Phillips.

My thanks to Ed Auerlich-Sugai and Tom Thompson for their help with angels.

I am grateful to my friends who critiqued one or more of the numberless drafts of this book: Kathleen Fraser, Bruce Boone, Carolyn Dinshaw, Edith Jenkins, Richard Schwarzenberger, Thom Gunn, Camille Roy, Carla Harryman, Bo Huston, Phyllis Taper, John Garrison, Kevin Killian, Aaron Shurin, Lydia Davis, Clara Sneed, Chris Komater, and Earl Jackson, Jr.

Thanks to *Mirage Period(ical)* and *Five Fingers Review* for publishing excerpts from this work.

Finally, my thanks to the Djerassi Foundation and to the MacDowell Colony for their support.

for Camille Roy, Angela Romagnoli, and Reese Romagnoli

And then too you must shape in your mind some people, people well-known to you, to represent for you the people in the Passion.... When you have done this, putting all your imagination into it, then go into your chamber. Alone and solitary, excluding every external thought from your mind...moving slowly from episode to episode, meditate on each one, dwelling on each single stage and step of the story.

—The Garden of Prayer
written for young girls in 1454

PART ONE
The Rule of L.

I am thy loue & shal be thy loue wyth-owtyn ende.

I

Can I interpret Love's canceled flights with only the language of canceled flights, his delayed arrivals with the language of delay?

In the 1430s, Margery Kempe wrote the first autobiography in English. She replaced existence with the desire to exist. A man drew water from a well while a child played around its edge. Beyond the city walls lay square orchards, wattled enclosures, and sheep folds. Clear blue sky, whitish at the horizon.

The moment Margery felt a separate consciousness inside her body was overwhelmingly bizarre. The certainty of her own death swam through her. After the child was born, devils pawed at Margery and tossed her around. Devils opened their mouths—an exasperating nudity appeared. One demon knelt like a suitor; it caught her ankle and tears spurted from its round blue eyes. In the wheedling voice of burlesque piety it implored Margery to deny God and the saints, her mother and father, and her own self. Margery tore the skin on her breast. She lost faith in the world and shrieked a tilted laugh. What sane person could afford such laughter? She roared at her husband John and her neighbors. Her periods stopped; her saliva tasted bitter. She wanted to kill herself and be reconceived in hell and as proof she bit so deep into her palms that crescents remained there for the rest of her life. Finally John tied her up.

Half yer viii wekys & odde days later, as Margery wrote, she lay so wide awake in the early dawn that the outside was pushed into sleep. She couldn't move; she was united with the weak light that passed through her shutters and glinted on coins, gleamed on a latch. She heard rustling from above, the bare feet of servants, and a magpie's rasping chatter.

Jesus was sitting next to her. He was birdlike, with a short pointed nose and complete arches over his eyes. He had bone-tipped shoulders and she recognized in his ideal posture and long neck her own "hidden" aristocracy. Sandy brown hair fell across his lofty forehead but he was a blond. His beauty seemed intentional because she desired it. He wore a short purple tunic. Tiny pink nipples were visible on his milky breast.

Jesus gazed up past his brow at Margery. His irises were disorganized blue geodes. He had been crying all weekend—it was Monday morning and he was still crying. He whispered, "I'm so abandoned." He raised his head in sadness and his face held the slow joy of deep sky above the sun.

He stood and turned on the balls of his feet and began to ascend. Margery fell half asleep when she saw the deity turn away. She felt the strongest sensation of her life, a welling of aspiration and desire embodied in the blur of dusty gold, the long smeared shadow of neck and spine, his broad hips, the semicircles of his ass, his long slightly knock-kneed legs. He rotated near the ceiling; she became conscious of the weight of her breasts and the hair down her back. The splayed tips of his long toes floated past her eyes. He raised his arm as darkness closed in. Later she concluded he was pointing to heaven.

Margery's ropes lay unknotted. She climbed out of bed and pulled back the heavy shutters. It was not dawn at all—plain light flooded the room without fanfare along with bird chatter and salty wind. An afternoon in Lynn, 1396.

2

Margery and John lay in a high bed covered in blue buckram with blue hangings. She raised her watery eyes as though someone were walking across the roof. She had opened a brewery in Lynn; it failed in four years. John snored a faint rasp and wind sighed in the reed beds. Encountering resistance, Margery regrouped and set a higher goal. She became a miller and failed even sooner.

John snored lightly; he was ten years older than Margery. He had auburn hair, thick arms and thighs. The hair on his chest was black cashmere, the nipples hard to find. His hair was part of the darkness.

John gathered the covers in sleep and bunched them under his chin. Margery listened; behind her boredom, a wash of ecstasy. She heard *along with* the silence and snoring a delectable music. Margery was thirty-one and Jesus was thirteen years younger; his welling choir cheered in her body. Flames from the pit of her stomach fanned through joints and membranes, a suggestion of wings in brilliant cobalt space, fiery stars where bodies should have been. John raised his big head reluctantly as Margery jumped down from their bed, shouting: *"Ecstasy in heaven!"*

Margery sewed a hairshirt into her dress to pitch herself to the edge of exasperation. She kept nothing else secret, talking to relive her intensity: *Je* pushed out, then *sus*, inward and under her tongue. She repeated *bliss* and *ecstasy*, words that looked beautiful in books by St. Bridget and St. Catherine. She'd had no peace of mind to begin with and she was not able to imagine a break from the world she knew.

At that time there were three popes. The financial control of the world and eternity was up for grabs, so people were burnt to discourage personal reckonings of experience. People of humble birth were vulnerable. Margery was not eager to die; she did not want liberation but a cosmic shortcut, the satisfaction of a greed for more life.

Margery spent two years in a state of arousal and despair. Jesus was a wish. She waited actively as though feeling the air quicken before rain, imminent saturation. His translucent skin—a milky wash over a base coat of gold dust. She conjured long conversations tremulous with sincerity and avowal—or he was describing her to Mary or God. She sat up and looked around, surprised he didn't appear in the creak of an opening door. She debated with bent treetops and the motionless bright horizon where clouds streamed into the sky. Her feet rubbed together, her tongue and mouth tingled, her membranes clanged with emptiness.

Margery was caught in the prison of six or seven positions, repeated hopelessly through the night. She expected compensation for the pain of his absence. Her excitement was sickening against the gray dawn and the house sparrows' insipid chirps.

She watched the world take shape. On her neighbor's roof a young man carried slate tiles up to his boss, his father possibly. Every time the young man laid down the stones, he hitched up his hose on his hipless torso and looked in her window.

They were separated by a few yards. He was shirtless; it was late July but it would not be hot for a few hours. His chest was smooth and white though he worked in the sun. He had long muscles in his arms and back, and black curls above a long haggard face. Swallows whose nests he had disturbed darted around him, shrilling *tsink, tsink, tsink.* She brought back a pear to bed and cut slices; the pear was crisp, with more fragrance than flavor. Margery liked her rosy curves and caverns and strength: she outdistanced John going uphill. The roofer whistled to get her attention.

Later she found him in front of her house wearing his doublet and apron. She imagined blunt acts. Above these fantasies, Jesus's face pitched in amazed spasms. She asked, "Do you know Jesus?"

The roofer stood with his legs apart. On the job his body felt efficient, concise; confronted by someone who expressed herself with a flourish and rich intonation, he was rooted to the spot. "If we don't fuck now, we'll do it later." He didn't even whisper.

Margery saw him at St. Margaret's that evensong. She was the daughter of the mayor. She wore a horned headdress of gold pipes with a wired-up veil. Her hair was entirely hidden; her hairline, eyebrows, and temples were plucked to produce a broad forehead. Margery identified with fabrics: she wore a cranberry silk gown with a flat white collar and trailing funnel-shaped sleeves, cinched above the waist with a soft milk-chocolate belt.

The roofer lounged against the west wall, waiting for Margery, one leg crossed over the other. He wanted to be typical, alienated under the eye of his master. Margery's longing for existence took the form of obsessive sexuality. The roofer was fifteen years old, so young his orgasms didn't matter. She re-aimed her entire self at a mercer she used to know. His shoulders were wide, his face heavy with problems, and when he came he hooted softly like an owl.

Margery lost the game of temptation as soon as she began to view her desire from every angle. If Jesus had not abandoned her, would she be so vehemently attracted? The silk moving around her body created an environment to walk through. The mercer grinned foolishly, looking right and left of a well-to-do woman of thirty-three with ruddy skin, a broad face, light-blue pop eyes, a turned-up nose, and small teeth. She was short but her eyes sought relation. He ran a finger down the crest of her nose and turned away.

As though completing one gesture, Margery hurried to bed, plowed through the night, and jumped up next morning. When she found the roofer her face sank in lust, her mouth an O. She asked him directly to have sex. "I'd rather be chopped up for stew-meat in a pot," he drawled with lazy malice. A wave of nausea warped the air around her. With a nod Margery understood that failure was intrinsic, success merely an exception.

3

L.'s summer house on Cape Cod: we choose a little square room—the only bedroom that has heat. Midmorning, early spring. The heater produces a tropical climate. L. kneels on the bed and I stand behind him. Veins run beneath the skin of his white-gold limbs like the web in insect wings. I draw his bony jaw over his shoulder and we kiss, then I withdraw except where we are joined. His own humility excites him. The motion of his ass makes me simple. Its hunger seems ageless. I raise my fingers in amazement. I'm entirely awake, all systems go. My skin intensifies as though the front of my body whirls. Incredibly, he whispers "Hold me," and I caress his chest and belly as he comes.

Later he drives me to Logan Airport. Wipers have left semicircles of dirt on the windshield of his Rabbit. We are speeding—late for my plane—but our sex has made us horny and I want to squeeze orgasms out of him. We pull off the highway and park, wriggle through a wire fence, and trek into a young forest of birch and pine. The woods look oddly beat up, broken branches strew the ground. We stop in a clearing that seems more pressured.

"Well..." He cocks his head in mild amusement. His features are a landscape that invites keenness of sight in that each element—cloud, lake, tree—tips towards me. He's the perfection of my type: a waif who dominates. We hear the harsh *cheet-cheet* of a crossbill. It's an honor to unbutton his pants. A page of porn lies at our feet—a faded torso, her thighs akimbo in the dirt. In all the miles of highway and forest we chose a chosen spot. I'm so drunk with love that coincidence rings with purpose. When L. blows me, wind in the treetops links it to fate. Then we kiss while he jacks us off; I expose my tongue and cock to the cool air.

We are extremely late but rigid beneath thin red skin. My orgasm is a small surprise, like stepping on a stick till it cracks. I come as easily as I blush. Inconsequential drops fall on the soft earth. L. bends over, pumping the log between his legs, eyebrows raised and jaw thrust forward as though he's riding a bike. I want his orgasm: he comes long ropy strings. I want to throw my head into the branches in repulsion and gratitude. I want to surround him but hold back, subsiding, feeling a little seedy.

I reach across distance—when I see L.'s handwriting my senses jump. His script resembles mine (that's a good sign); it has more velocity, more space between words.

Dear Bob,

Spending the weekend with G.'s parents during my favorite time of year. House wrens warble like crazy, their songs bubbling out from under the eaves, the air muffled under the shifting beech, elm, and honey locust. Sumptuous dinners, interesting company—I feel more comfortable here than in my parents' home—this is so much more the way they are supposed to live. A pack of corgies tumbling around the house, beautiful antiques from some great-aunt that are slightly beaten up, parents who are well-read, excellent hosts. And sensing also how this very graciousness muffles some adventurousness (or perhaps curiosity to absorb contradictions and accept the incompleteness of our century), realizing how I feel slightly more capable of doing so. Blessing or booby prize? Thinking about sucking your nipples and developing new fetishes.

XOXOXOXO *The Nurse of Love*

His letter doesn't console me for his absence because it conveys little interest in seeing me, just in being seen: his melancholy, his beautiful youth. I shrug, weakened, empty of promise. I'm still in bed; it's rush hour, eight in the morning. Cars boom as they pass below my window. No one knows what I put into my waiting.

I read his letter again, wondering how to match my charming, horny correspondent, whose wit enters from the side, with the man whose attributes I analyze in a plenitude that goes against understanding, naming them as reverently as a god's—silky, strong, frail. What characterizes a god?

His larger existence, an imperative that meaning stay with him, the mobility to retreat from the deep surrender he inspires. He governs my fantasies—his golden face convulses as it never does. I rustle and groan, a shallow orgasm with his approval in the form of his arousal. As I age I clench over my spasms instead of arching backwards from them. His naked skin expresses mortality and compassion. My last word when I die will be his name—to say it in the *grandest* setting.

I need L. to be only mine; for that to happen I must exhibit him and my desire. I call Tom, I call Kathy, I call my old friend Ed. In the theaters of their consciousness I stage my drama. That my love for L. is possible, actual. That my joy exists. Interaction shifts the ground of the finite. They create belief by responding to my story when I meet them in cafés, on street corners, on the phone; Margery turns the cosmos into the witness of her love.

Ed is breathless; he will die before long and I feel ruthless using up his strength, but he listens to my boastful grievances and amazement. (I kept Margery in mind for twenty-five years but couldn't enter her love until I also loved a young man who was above me.) L. won't say *I miss you*. He did say *I love you*. He gives me clothes and presents whose accuracy is a higher form of speech. His family acts without prudery, naked all day above the servants, grooming each other at the lake. I wake at night expecting L. to be in my bed in San Francisco. His rich person's problems create a mood of unreality even in himself. I know him, his dilemmas—does that oppress him?

Ed is still listening. He says, "L.'s features are so polished, they're almost overdone." I eagerly agree. L. is wide open, tender, remote, precise, serious, unsure... First I fought for meaning, now I have too much of it. I disappear from a position too full or empty to reveal the extent of my need. I'm Margery following a god through a rainy city. The rapture is mine, mine the attempt to talk herself into existence.

4

Margery prayed on the stone floor of a side-chapel at St. Margaret's the Friday before Christmas, 1406; little statues made of rye dough adorned the altar. She prayed on one knee, arms outstretched like a crucifix. Jesus delayed and Margery was weary, overcome by desire. She thought her suffering was the result of bad luck which good luck could reverse. Daydreams of acknowledgment took shape in the beyond. A priest, young and handsome, held the sacrament over his head. A keening in his chest never stopped. The sacrament *shok & flekeryd to & fro*, as Margery wrote— a white dove calling *turrr turrr* and batting its wings as blue sky burst through the roof.

Jesus pictured Margery carrying fruit in her apron in a small orchard her family owned behind her house: she's squinting in the sun and he can smell her sweat. They roll on top of hard pears. She laughs at moments that surprise him—her irony frames these wholesome images.

When he returned to Margery it was nothing like that. He materialized, barefoot on the wood, goosebumps on his thighs and arms. She had not seen him for ten years. His hair was browner than she remembered. He wore a sweet gaunt smile that pulled downwards, and his skin moved her with the fact of his birth. Margery's round face surged forwards; her eyes sought to rush him over the bridge they created. Her love of his fresh body was accompanied by—even based on—a horror of decay. He stepped backwards into the table in Margery's bedroom. Jesus had L.'s Scottish face—high narrow brow with smooth features crowded beneath, eyebrows defined more by delicate bones than hair.

The table dented the flesh of his ass and, as he turned, the long nape of his neck discharged a jolt of beauty in Margery. She fell to her knees. He felt he had done enough, that she had altered the situation—perhaps unfairly—by needing to give all her love away.

Jesus's strong sense of occasion took over. He knelt and kissed her, pleasure needling his inner walls. He whispered her name. Once sex was entered, his eyes shut and his mouth gaped like a baby bird's. Margery struggled between closing her eyes and gazing through the bony architecture of his face to its virginal dazzle.

When Jesus slid his finger into Margery, he knew she'd had lots of penetration. They had the same smell—a good sign. It's obvious when men become aroused; women must be expressive: she threw her head from side to side.

They pushed fingers inside each other and strummed as though trying notes till they located the nerve of an exact turmoil: the frazzled eyes and slack jaws. They gazed at the dire implosions that half belong to the one who causes them. Jesus's asshole seemed like a flaw that drew her attention more than the beauty it marred, till finally the flaw became an expression of herself by dint of her struggle. She fingerfucked him urgently. "Slow down." His mild voice came from his other end. She rotated the finger. *Ummmm*—a sound to revive later in the distance.

Jesus was the world and Margery rode panting on top. He spread her lips far apart until her clit rubbed against him. A thrill lit its tip and burned into her belly. The orgasm pushed her features as though she were traveling into a strong wind. The past slid away from the wealth of the present, sheen and felicity that can't be saved. The muscles in his long passive legs reacted to pleasure with little twitches. "I spasmed eleven times," he mused. He'd been counting absentmindedly. He withdrew slowly, a shiny slug. He was beginning to depend on Margery; she had more faith in him than he had in himself.

"Be thankful, St. Bridget never saw me fluttering like a dove."

"What does it mean?" Jealousy kept her alert.

"Tell whoever you wish: I turn your heart upside down." Margery was thrilled; she rippled, sucking him back in, released from the prison of striving simply by getting what she wanted. She tightened her grip and foamy syrup seeped out. He added, "You're pregnant."

She had already guessed—her breasts were swollen and she was often tired. "Who will look after this child?"

"I'll arrange it." She awakened his self-esteem. He took in her naked body and billowing red hair. Her nipples were raw, exposed, sensitive as foreskin. He said, "We look like statues."

Margery considered his broad hips and jumble of limbs. She said, "One goddess and one cow dropped from heaven."

Her insult was an experiment; he laughed and drew her down as though they were a couple.

Snow fell during the night. Jesus woke with a hard-on so powerful it clunked when Margery rapped it. He said, "Here's a penny from my heart to put in your purse." In the midst of scalding pleasure her eyes opened on a patch of his skin bunched between her thumb and finger, and she was held by its fine wrinkles. Later they looked out at the white hush; they thought about breakfast. It burned to piss. Her skin wrinkled, her stomach swelled, her navel flattened, silvery stretch marks appeared on her belly.

5

The following August, a few weeks after the baby was born, Jesus asked Margery to go with him to Norwich to meet the Vicar of St. Stephen's. Travel would come to equal the adventure of loving him. He strode ahead on long legs as though leading a troupe, making decisions without her, his nose in the air, turning down lanes past carts loaded with grain, dung, or salt from the local salt pans. Cottages stood vacant, emptied by plague. Fields of lavender bloomed with lilting fragrance in the clayey soil.

Jesus had the forward stiff-legged gait of an athletic woman. He wore a short green brocade gown with bagpipe sleeves and a high dagged collar; his beaver hat was lined with vermilion velvet and bore a plume of gold threads. His feet felt cunning in expensive boots; like other rich people, he was pious about such luxuries and thought their excellence was a kind of justice in itself. His tall figure stood out in fantastic elegance against fields and open heaths.

Margery followed on short legs in cheaper shoes, wearing a mantle of black wool. Her breath whistled and a stitch rode high in her side. The lane was deeply rutted and in places centuries of traffic had worn through the strata of freestone so it looked more like a water course bedded with naked rag. Her shoes were ponderous with gray mud. A partridge called in the fields, a high creaking *keeve, keev-it, it, it, it*. Jesus did not slow down on hills. "Why are you walking so fast?" He looked back, eyebrows raised.

The world was spread out, offered to the view. The sun was at the meridian; to the south the heaths glared through yellow steam. A blond dog too old to chase the grazing hares barked at them with joy, each bark so full it lifted the front of her body off the ground. She was broad abeam and trotted alongside Margery and Jesus on stiff arthritic legs. She caught Margery's eye, a gleeful camaraderie.

The dog tried to keep up, panting and thrusting her neck forwards as though she were pulling a cart. For *her* Jesus slowed down on the inclines; he called her Pooch-kins—exasperating. Margery was thirteen years older than Jesus and she had just given birth. She felt explosions in her chest. A nimbus of gnats and horseflies wailed around her perishable face, the face of Thumbelina drawn with the burnt tip of a match. Her suffering didn't diminish her desire for Jesus—confusion implied more life.

Near dusk Norwich rose out of bedrock, a hat on a table—its spires, walls, guildhalls, minster clock, and castle—so clean it moved towards them on the plain. Merchants and farmers streamed through the city gate; a peasant drove a pig from market with a goad, the peasant's alcoholic face so bright with need that Margery responded with unwilling arousal; a blind man begged on the grass; a young woman stared shyly at the retreating back of a lady with coiled yellow hair—she wanted to press that lady's low-slung breasts together and suck both nipples at once. The lady was escorted by a cavalier on whose wrist perched a kestrel with a blue-gray head and spotted chestnut mantle.

Norwich was in the midst of a summer festival. Doorways were decorated with Saint-John's-wort, lilies, and lanterns hung to burn all night. Near the bonfires wealthy citizens set meat and drink for their neighbors. The streets were so crowded that any cranny of emptiness was immediately filled by bodies and going forwards a few yards was a victory.

Margery and Jesus breathed air dense with sweat and perfume; they felt touched by the ephemeral: they had remarkably similar takes on goods and people, the jugglers and the bear. When they last saw Poochkins she was at attention, transfixed by a rib roast on a plank, eyes misty and tail rotating behind. Jesus said, "Her hunger seems ageless." She ignored their calls.

On Thursday a little before noon Margery entered St. Stephen's. The Vicar wore a mantle of fine black shank. He sat down with her in the church. Coins from his purse dropped onto the back of his chair. As he stood to collect them his gloves fell out of his lap. As he bent to retrieve them his glasses fell off. Margery covered her face—she felt wind on her nipples though she was wearing a wool gown.

She was nervous. "Jesus told me to speak with you."

"Explain that," the Vicar said.

So Margery began telling him about the time she first saw Jesus, gaining courage as she felt the potential rise in her clear voice: her vanity, her obstinacy, her envy, her horrible temptations. The Vicar was gaining weight; he was aware of his belly bulging against his chest and his breasts drooping onto the skin beneath. He wondered if Margery was conscious of her body touching itself there or her cunt lips touching each other.

When she spoke of Jesus, the ground emitted organ music that seemed to have a shouting crowd in it; vibrations weakened her arms and legs. She lay still for a long time, then told the Vicar he would die in nine years. "The warning is that your nose will bleed: in three days you will be stark dead." The Vicar sat with his hands folded, too amazed to move. He felt dead already and abandoned the sense of going forwards, and he wondered how others sustain the momentum to plan their tombs.

Margery recounted conversations with Jesus more exalted than *Stimulus Amoris* or *Incendium Amoris*. She had a rare rose and there were not enough ears in the world to hear of the paradise of its bloom.

The Vicar saw himself twisted and crumpled forwards although he sat immobile; he wished for silence. All his appetite and striving would come to nothing. It dawned on him that he didn't know himself, had never taken the trouble because it meant facing all his sluggish, stubborn unhappiness. That he didn't like himself, wasn't likable. She showed him the cries and gestures—inordinate sobbing, *Have mercy, Jesus* and *I die*—how people slandered her, claiming a spirit tormented her, or that she was sick.

6

My book depends on the tension between maintaining an impersonation and breaking it—I interject an aside *in the deepest possible voice:* L. and I were introduced in 1987 by mutual friends when L. considered moving to San Francisco. It was raining. He sat on my Mission chair with his arms crossed, and I wondered actively what it was like to be blond and lanky and withheld. I began an examination of L. which came to equal my own aims and ends. I had been alone for four years—so lonely I was afraid. I was about to turn forty and he was twenty-six.

In clothes he was blank but during our first lovemaking he clung for dear life. We clung to each other. I laughed with confusion when he confessed he was extremely rich. When I describe L. my language is sleepy—I can't wake it up.

My love for L. restored a faith that had become as polluted as the air and water. He wrote, "After meeting you in January, I went out again to reclaim my history, my relationships, things that define me. Your attention forced this blossoming. My feeling of belonging in New York has revived."

Huge days and nights. Movement is pointless; sight is muddy. I can only believe that the force of my waiting will change him. I hear—even before L.'s greeting—the echo and hiss of a long-distance connection. Then I know the taste of victory and joy rains down like ticker tape on that narrow electrical street.

I make two wishes: to be L.'s lover and to have the freedom to write. I wait a moment for the wishes to come true; at the end of the moment I am older and so separate from others that I feel mutilated. L.'s voice is bright, charming the distance away. "What's new and different?" His tone assumes it's obvious to both of us that he can't be with me.

I complain about my job—demanding, exhausting. He says, "Possession of a condom in a New York jail is a misdemeanor. The commissioner says they can be filled with sand and used as weapons." L. has joined ACT UP and does AIDS graphics. I encourage, approve—he needs some human scale in his life. I also take part in political demonstrations, but I aim my desire for freedom at myself and L. in the form of total arousal. As though one thought leads to the next he says he's trying to establish a connection with his father. I wish all his efforts would lead to me. He asks after my dog Lily, gentle and foggy in old age.

In his absence I lose track of who he is, in the psychological sense. I abandon my ordinariness and leave the rickety shelter of my own self which, being vacant, attracts ghosts and obsessions. On Valentine's Day a card arrives: almost identical black-and-white photos printed vertically on glossy paper. He stands with his back to the camera, wearing only black socks; he holds up a flag of black cloth by its corners so his body glows in front. Long nape, intricate shoulders, narrow back, and simple semicircles of his butt. He stitched hearts into both images with red thread; the hearts outline and frame the blank slate of his ass. *from L. (aka Tabula Rasa)* XOXOXO—

7

Jesus lowered his eyes and said, "Like a mother I give you my breast to suck." The strongest wave of life's attraction to itself carried Margery forwards. She gazed at his chest, smooth and eventless as a teenager's, and at his tiny nipples, expecting a miracle: she attained the rhapsodic mobility of the wealthy and immortal—the time and allowance to travel. Her ecstasy was so condensed she felt separate from the moment, ready to faint.

As though to amplify the theme of breast feeding, Jesus asked Margery to help nurse him. Margery felt residual twinges of pleasure; she heard the whickering trill of a grebe. She moved through the resistance of time—her mantle billows backwards into the future as her forehead met the past.

It's painful that I can't be present in every moment of L.'s life. Margery saw the sky, landscape, architectural background, then foreground, figures, heads, and faces. She moved through divided space to warm linen by the fire with other servants.

Jesus's mother was slim, with bright gold hair, delicate hands, and her son's tall forehead. Mary had barely materialized and spoke in rushed whispers. Margery bent towards her. "Executioners were naked... A tavern nearby... In those days... Yellow awning when the heat... Little tavern made clams... With plenty of..." Mary wrinkled her forehead, expecting an answer to a hard question; her face suffused with tenderness as though the answer had been given.

Joseph wore a peaked turban to emphasize the oriental locale. He danced a jig as a little mess of a cat attacked his ankles. Mary's robe was so thin her swollen belly was visible. "The angel's shadow startled me. Plaid mantle and a... bronze..." She was sensitive to color as a defense against sadness; she wished her periods would stop. A desert finch lit at their feet and took its ten or twelve positions in the twinkling of an eye.

Margery led Mary and Joseph towards Bethlehem. They couldn't reach town in time so they camped in an abandoned stable whose thatched roof was supported on one side by a stone wall and on the other by the rooted trunk of a dead cypress. They were filthy, tired, and hungry. Joseph tethered the ox and donkey and set a taper between the stones that spilled its thick flame upwards. He went to the city to find a midwife.

Margery removed Mary's shoes and veil. Mary raised her palms in piety and her belly moved. She felt contractions in her back rather than her stomach. Pushing

Jesus out was like shitting, but euphoria replaced that feeling the instant he was born.

When Joseph returned with two midwives Margery had already cut the tiny umbilical cord with her dagger. The two women took the liberty of confirming Mary's virginity. They were somber and amazed, their wimples and veils made of thick black fustian.

"St. Andrew took his clothes off...gave them to his executioner..." Mary's blathering was an unbreakable silence. Margery wondered, Is the whole family simple-minded? She snatched up the baby, who seemed to need her, and wrapped him *in fayr whyte clothys & kerchys* that she had brought along.

There was no pain or blood, little to hinder Mary's descent from vision to daydream. She seemed to forget about her son on his birthday. The virgin-mother contradiction was only medical; she didn't feel like a virgin *or* a mother. For her the body already hung upside down, flayed and exposed. She rejected subject matter per se, even though Jesus had palmed Margery off on her.

Margery found them lodgings in Bethlehem. Mary and Joseph squatted naked, combing each other for nits, cracking lice between fingernails. Physical life was new to the gods; deity had no shame. The tips of Mary's nipples were long and Joseph's cock was a length of rotten rope below a pad of gray curls. Being human was a costume party—dressing up in flesh and blood. All they brought was hard bread and a pot of stale beer so Margery made a soup called beer-bread.

8

John caressed Margery on April 26, 1413. By then Margery had fourteen children and that's as much as she tells us about them. It was a fresh watery afternoon. It moved John that her cunt was a soft-lipped entrance at the very bottom of her torso, just where he desired it to be. He lay his head on her chest. When he touched her clit it replied with heartbeats. He gained color and reality. He always forgot and then recognized the smell of apricots in the sweat between her breasts; he tended her nipples—in exciting them he made himself writhe and moan.

Margery knew what kind of sex John wanted—recognition, perfection of the moment—because she sought it herself with Jesus. Sadly she turned from John by closing her eyes, refusing to honor their arousal or make it symbolic. Through her pleasure she screamed *"Jesus, help me!"* and John's erection melted. John became fixed, two dimensional. He blew and fluttered, splayed open, tearing into ragged pieces with a tender hapless expression. What a mess, Margery said to herself.

At the market in Bethlehem, the vegetable woman threw carrots, celery, parsley, and a head of garlic into the meagerest purchase. Margery raised her hands for more and became that gesture. The odd shape of her packages forced her to hurry.

She added cold to the tub and sprinkled a few drops on her wrist. Jesus splashed and clapped, soaking

Margery while she kissed a tiny to-be-wounded foot. "I will not bind you too tight—I know your painful death." The prick of the milk on Margery's nipple, her bliss, the sore and swollen feeling as milk engorged each breast, her sadness preceding the arrival of the little teeth. Tears flowed as though she could never die.

Joseph complained, "Be still, daughter." Margery smoothed their sheets and raised her cracked bowl to strangers.

Even in her own visions the gods ignored Margery while she found lodging for them every night and begged for white clothes for Jesus. The humming in her ear grew deep, an owl's *oo-heu*, and brighter, a bunting's high-pitched jangle. She leaned over the fire, stirring milk and barley as Mary's brittle fingers drifted through loose galaxies above the bubbling cauldron. Mary's nails were cracked and dirty. Her blue mantle of Flanders cloth hugged her shoulders, fell in large bowl shapes to her waist, then straight downwards. She lifted the corner elegantly; the weighty abundance of folds expressed feminine eternity while her body inside remained untouched.

Jesus didn't want his afternoon nap. The sun beat through the shades. A quiver of pleasure and then the current running through his little cock entertained him. The air was so hot his piss didn't cool off. He filled his diaper and painted a mural with shit to surprise his mother. Mary leaned close to the wall and sniffed—then threw her head back and sputtered with laughter.

An angel hurtled out of the blue. It glided over the ground towards the family, its silver wings slightly canted and sharp as scissors. "Look out," Joseph squawked, "in two seconds they'll cut your head off." Their clothes caught the wind and puffed out as the angel skidded to a halt. Its lips were parted and it breathed through its mouth from exertion.

The angel cried, "Mary and Joseph, go to Egypt." The ground was bare and the road hard and dry; grass sprouted from clefts in the rocks. Mary stopped to rest, dangling Jesus upside down from her lap. He watched a trader lead a string of ostriches that were bridled and saddled. His heart thudded in his ears. There was a fragrance in the air like sage, hot and dry, that would always turn him upside down again. Margery wrung her hands and wept slowly for hours at a time.

9

Jesus, when I feel the difference between my stale life and the ecstasy of life with you, I revive the desolation I felt before meeting you in order to coax your appearance. I begin crying so intently my voice sounds hoarse and strange. My face is rigid, my arms and legs are weak, and civilization grows tender and sensitive to pain. There is a bleating in my chest, a sixth sense, the continuous awareness of your body. I enlarge myself by equating your tenderness towards me with the pain of your death. My jaws lock open and tears and mucus spool off my face.

I'm on my stomach in a side chapel at St. Margaret's. My hipbones press against the floor, gas moves through the side of my gut, my hot cheek grinds on the stone. My crying is choked; I curl into a ball and clench, an impossible shape. I put myself in your body. Its frequency is so high it heaves upwards. You need me as you did at first.

Into our most intense union the opposite feeling enters—disorder, the strangeness of what's happening to me. Tears don't stop but convulsions do. The more I need you, the deeper the estrangement, the stronger my desire—a defect in the movement of love.

I'm so tired of being alone. I swim through my tears to the back of my head to observe this, my crying regular as a swimmer's breath. That retreat allows ghosts to enter: you stumble towards me as a rickety man, one leg keeps caving in; you say with complete understanding, "If it weren't for my body I could go on forever." We fall into each other's arms and as we grieve I rejoice, a welling feeling of life which now even pain stimulates. I become aroused as a flat sweet odor makes my gorge rise. I promise that I will save you—your eyes darken and your face rolls away. The stench of decay spreads as I make the pledge. Your tongue is stiff as the metal clapper of a bell, purple-brown like burnt iron. Everything wasted. I witness my anguish with excitement—who would reject *more life?*

In my bleak monotonous weeping, I wonder at the very terms of suffering's argument: that you *are*, my love *is*, you *die*, flesh *is*—a baffling confirmation—it's not *pain* or *joy* until wept out as *fiery tears.* That outburst causes a tooth of pleasure to bite hard. Currents travel through me to the distance. When I finish crying I'm empty, exalted.

Withdraw my tears and I do not enjoy food, drink, or talk; there is no flavor until I weep again.

10

A moonless night, the snow frozen over so our footsteps crunch. A fifth of B&B stands in my pocket. The waterfall doesn't make a sound—a huge sheet of mid-flight ice. L.'s flashlight beam finds an oval that melted or never froze and through that hole we see a black torrent endlessly spill. L.'s voice says, "It's frightening." Why is that, I wonder?

We share the flask, a mouthful of potent fumy syrup. I lean out of the light against a trunk, sluggish with the desire to be kissed. Cold lips, tongue fiery with brandy. His fragile heat is a dull fear embedded in deep winter. "Too bad life isn't a cafeteria: pay first, eat without dreading the bill."

"No," he answers, "the cost is so appalling you couldn't stand the food." I'm impressed by his bitterness, a moment of harmony between us. The beam picks out the hole which conveys a beckoning vitality—the rictus of a corpse announcing that the present is dead.

When Margery prayed for confirmation of her union with Jesus, she heard a loud rumbling. A stone and a chunk of wood dislodged from under a rafter of St. Margaret's vault. They hovered, each rotating on its own. The stone fell on Margery's head with a crack and the wood struck her back with a thud. His cruelty offered a breach through which to hurl herself into the fullness of life. She staggered forwards and sprawled on the floor, screaming, *"Mercy, Jesus!"*

Master Allyn, a doctor of divinity at Cambridge and an indexer of miracles and prophecies, arrived next day and weighed the stone: 3 lbs., June 12, 1413. (During puberty Master Allyn resented nature when it fiddled with his body: the real past under the official one.) He snatched the beam end out of the fire: 6 lbs. He pursed his lips as he measured Margery's head, "to do a service for eternity." She became aware of her breasts hanging foolishly.

Margery invited Master Allyn to dinner—bream from the Fens. He took a bite and looked down at a pamphlet but never finished reading a sentence because his eyes returned too quickly to the food. He was unique, a perfect example of a type. Margery laughed: there's something juvenile about striving so explicitly to be an intellectual. Master Allyn was stiff as a board; his ponderous explanations affected everyone. Later John did an impression. "Master Allyn, Master Allyn, first you *squeeeeze* your *asshole,*" and he jerked upright.

John was happy; he couldn't see what was in store. He wore his hair short for his class as though rejecting ambition and his smile was intense, a child's drawing, all teeth. He put his huge arms around his wife while she averted her face like a face card and folded her hands, touching only herself. She couldn't marry Jesus till she freed herself from John and obtained a license to dress in white like a saint.

Margery needed to be heard to shore up her own belief in herself. She and John went to Canterbury looking for people in authority to help her advance as a saint and avoid being burnt as a Lollard. The Lollards were a sect that attacked the corrupt clergy. They rejected miracles and stressed missionary work, making converts as they preached from village to village. Margery brought to the countryside only the drama of her romance with Jesus. The Lollards were a sign of the times; next year, in 1414, they would attempt a revolution.

Margery lived during the Hundred Years War, the collapse of feudal systems, and the plague. Towns had walls; at night the gates shut. At the beginning of modernity the world and otherworld lay in shambles. Margery was an individual in a recognizable nightmare: the twentieth century will also be called a hundred years war. A simpler individual, she went by her first name except once before a high court. The same individual who now disintegrates. Inner life is a kind of greed, desire a form of personal profit. She pushes out of the flat pictorial plane into personality and suspense, illusion of escape, while I go back to the ruins of overall pattern and to the somber murmur of the already known.

Margery impressed Jesus who in turn motivated her. She challenged a monk in high office in Canterbury. "Sir, I accuse you of lechery, despair, and keeping worldly goods." She was assertive, credible. She stood too close, depriving him of the space he needed to marshal arguments.

(Three decades earlier, some men the monk met in a latrine invited him to a party. One of them had eaten a very hot meal with a lot of pepper. He asked, "Is that okay?" The monk didn't understand until he kissed the man, licked him, fucked him, found that every orifice was peppery, a prickly sensation, wildly stimulating. The man could twist into any position yet keep the monk's cock in his ass, heretic in a fire. The monk didn't know if his desire to be revealed in excitement could be touched let alone satisfied. His knees clamped together, then flew apart; his body arched backwards from his navel in a taut bow of flesh. The others stared in admiration. The odor of penetration, the serious air.)

The monk asked, "Say, with wives or single women?" He would not look at her directly.

"Neither, Sir."

The monk was fearful and assertive by turns. He followed Margery out. "We'll burn you, false Lollard. Here's a cartful of thorns ready for you, and a barrel to burn you with!" They had already burnt two heretics under barrels—their muffled screams remained in the square. Other people took up the cry, running to the scene, arms raised, and two boys started pelting Margery with mud.

Margery couldn't find John—he hated conflict. She fell to her knees and cried till her ribs hurt. "I cry your mercy, Jesus, for all my enemies, for all that are sick, for all lepers—" Sweat streaked her blue-as-lead face so the crowd recoiled in horror of disease. She prayed to keep them from everlasting damnation so they spat to scare the devil. The tide of belief was still high and few could wonder if Margery was fake. In her tears and threats the crowd caught a whiff of disaster that transcended everything.

A stocky black-whiskered man felt contempt for anything unusual. He pushed his sour face into Margery's. "We'll drown you in tears," his lifeless voice more frightening than screams. Two handsome men offered to escort her to her inn but Margery couldn't remember where it was, only that a German ran it. She wept so fiercely it was amazing that eyes survived or heart endured (heretic in flames).

II

The weather turned mushy, rosebuds rotted on the trellises. On June 23, Margery and John set off on a pilgrimage to Bridlington. They traveled through the Fens and then on a road through barley and rye fields cultivated for centuries. The grain was just coming into ear and the fields were dotted with vermilion poppies. Margery and John's brown ponies stepped reluctantly in the mud and sometimes stopped, eyes rolling in distaste.

A farmer planting winter forage followed his plow; his pubic hair itched and his muddy hose hung over the side of his hoggers. His wife walked ahead with a long goad; she wore a clouted coat cut short to the knee. A loose flock of blackbirds pecked at the newly sown seeds. She shrugged and remarked to the ox that it looked like rain. The road was lined with boulders that resembled huge slabs of marbled meat.

Another mile and the road divided. The landscape is my longing materialized; there is no more world; the sentence that describes landscape, clothes, and food goes nowhere—it's already aroused, a heaven where L. and I are making love. My lyricism is my tenderness for L.

On the corner stood a cottage next to a mountain of garbage; in the garden a girl scooped peat-black soil with a piece of slate. Her mother had been unable to satisfy a craving for oysters, so black oyster shells covered the child's hands and feet. Flowers and birds shone with individual life and identification with their species, an elaborate and finicky charm. A rufous woodcock flew fast and the undulating hills stretched back into unusual depth.

The pilgrims stopped near a roofless hut circled by the stone wall of a garden run wild. Wrens warbled and a small flock of goldfinches pecked along the hedgerows and cried *deedelit* from a patch of thistles. John stooped on a slimy footstone to drink from a well covered by ferns. He had little control over his life but in bed his confidence was magisterial. When he was sixteen his body had made itself known in a rush of exhilaration. He took long walks, had continuous sex, masturbated; he peaked for days and barely slept.

Margery, the more powerful citizen, became abandoned and frenzied in sex. She carried a bottle of ale and

John had a loaf tucked against his chest. John removed his riding huke and slung it over a branch. The somber buzzing insects made them aware of the silence.

When they had finished eating, John laid his head on Margery's chest, his throat extended, face tilted back. He was surprised by her heartbeat. His stomach felt tight; small signals beeped in his cock and thighs and merged with the lavish ache of needing to shit. He was clinging to the moment. Soft heat raked the treetops, the sharp tang of resin and a woodwarbler's shivering call. "If a man with a sword chopped off my head unless we made love..."

Margery protested, "We've been chaste eight weeks."

". . . . . ."

"I would rather *se thow be slayn*," as Margery wrote.

Shock raised John's eyebrows. He considered the endless renewable pleasure in her nipples; their aureoles were wide, a wealth of dark-pink tissue. He had a friendly attitude towards humanity.

"When we touch, I get so scared I'm paralyzed. You're a dragon, a fire breather."

"Admit it," she laughed, "I shed more water than fire."

"It's the beer."

Margery snorted, "Through my *eyes.*"

She looked at John; he was recognizable. Margery found she was a tourist at heart; without a backward glance she abandoned a sex life most people would be grateful for. She was tired of his hairy butt, his big feet, and the way he laughed with his mouth wide open. He was not satisfying to quarrel with since he didn't mind being wrong.

As though defending himself, John cried, "How can you be a teacher when you never *listen?*"—a strange grievance since he didn't speak for hours on end. "Grant my desires and I'll grant yours. First, sleep with me in one bed. Second, pay my debts. Third, eat and drink with me on Friday." He held a petty municipal office; their money came from her side of the family.

"No, I'll never break my fast." But John lost the contest by offering to negotiate. He wore the pleading expression and searching eyes of a beggar. Margery was moved and slightly repelled. His humility conveyed the depth of a love she was rejecting.

Jesus was a breath of crushed strawberries: "That's why I ordered you to fast—to trade it for your chastity."

So Margery made a counteroffer. "If you take a vow of chastity at a bishop's hand, I will pay your debts and eat with you on Friday."

John's acceptance contained the end of his marriage, poverty, senility, and death.

12

Jesus was already more beautiful than a man could be, but Margery wanted to adorn him with her own grief in order to possess by giving. So it was a joy to be punished for speaking of Jesus; she wanted to be murdered for his sake. She imagined the easiest death so she wouldn't back down at the last moment: her head and feet were tied to a stake and her neck was severed with an axe so sharp she felt only the gust of an opening door. The blade flashed: a moment of elated appetite.

Jesus said "thank you" rather mildly. L.'s half-smile guarded Jesus's lack of definition; he would not be named by Margery's desire. He avoided her eye and, entering St. Margaret's, he slammed the wicket door in her face. It banged against her forehead and sent her staggering backwards down two stone steps into the airy summer morning. She was confused by her own unreality and broke into parts that looked around slackjawed as though they were in a strange place instead of a strange situation. She heard the crusty whistle of a hawk and slowly reunited in the blinking sunlight.

She found Jesus sitting in a dark side-chapel unwrapping a walnut cake. He offered some fondly as though he hadn't seen her in days. Margery loved pastry, loved to eat.

He said, "I have a late birthday gift for you." He stood and let his tunic drop to his feet. They both took in his clavicle's architecture, his solid belly with its tiny navel, the veins in his arms and legs. Margery wore a goofy grin. She liked skinny men and wanted to climb his body like a ladder. *Just a head, a cock, and a backbone to keep them apart.*

Jesus shoved two fingers between the lips of the wound in his side. He was not in pain; he aimed his tight excitement at Margery as he exposed himself. She responded with lust so direct it was also wonder. Jesus fished a blue cuff trimmed with vair from deep inside and continued pulling the sleeve and bodice till he yanked the entire garment free of his body and shook it out with a feeling of volume. He helped her on with it, a gown of heavy brocade, close-fitting right up to the chin.

She interpreted his gift as an apology because its blue matched her pale eyes. Between bites of the walnut cake she asked, "Why did you slam the door in my face?" The cake was sweetened with honey and figs, seedy and prickly on her tongue.

"I don't know," Jesus replied, as though that were an explanation. He smoothed the back of her gown and dropped to one knee. Margery saw the top, front, and rear of his skinny body, and his awkward position seemed to give her access. She could have raised him like a doll in the palm of her hand with the power of a tenderness that was avid, predatory. She wanted to suck his bones.

"It's a nice dress," Jesus stated. He was surprised—who questioned him this way? He basted the hem, pins held between lips, face tipped back from the conflict. If Jesus considered what was fair, where could he stop? He was the world: whatever he did was accurate.

His certainty compelled Margery. "Am I over-reacting?"

Jesus said regretfully, "There's nothing I can say." His small features vanished. His gift-giving retreat was an invitation to pursue. That made sense to Margery because his straight back and supple body were beyond her means. She wondered what his words meant detached from the clarinet of his voice.

"Tears are the most secure gift. No one can take them from you."

13

The thick drunken histamine ache of needing to shit; L. can't find a toilet in time; his face convulses; it makes me feel awe. Jesus doesn't have a conscience. Like L., whatever he does is normal.

I try to locate drama in L.'s face where drama is purposefully withdrawn. We look at art. We talk about neutral things. We visit old gardens where he identifies trees and flowers. We give each other rich objects produced for Edwardians which amplify my idea of him—extensions of desire and aspiration, like Mme. Arnoux's furniture and Mme. Bovary's clothes which Flaubert lovingly described.

My cousin says L. has an actor's voice. I think *beautiful, modulated*, but perhaps he means L. projects intimacy. L. says *"Bob"* rather than "hello." After a few moments with him, a friend whispers, "He's a cloud. If you push, he'll just disappear." How does she see that? L. speaks on any subject. I'm proud but critical: the world is his. He might leave his house, city, or country without his wallet or passport, while I check money and I.D. every few minutes. L. is prevented from renting a car because he forgot his license; when the manager sees L.'s family name, he restores L.'s exalted mobility.

I see my own inertia—I haven't budged for decades. L. snaps his fingers and we are standing on the terrace of a grand hotel, a blue view of mountains and ocean. It's not even visual—I *feel* my way across the landscape, the hard heat of youth.

L.'s relatives are the legendary robber barons, but he lives austerely, rich in feeling. He's hazy about his own money which he also regards as something to nurture. The importance of art, his lack of accomplishment, and the size of the art world overwhelm him. That's acceptable because he's so young. I can help with these problems.

Six A.M. We slide out of mist and cross a mirror lake; we whisper. L. is showing me a pair of loons he's watched for years. They are shy, eggs unguarded on the bare ground, tender hooting of ghosts, straw beaks.

Greed for more life spoils the life in front of me. I want promotion to the more real universe of freedom and protection from the bill. I can't strive anymore: we choose between the Adirondacks or the Cape, which would be *convenient*. My emotions lack precision—I "wake up" to the fear of death, the drive to be heard.

L. quotes my writing, yet now my lack of time to write seems like a character flaw, earning a living like the result of bad planning. My job puts me at the center of so much trouble that I never get out of the center. L. protests, "You only talk about yourself." He must have been patient for a long time.

He's warm in letters and on the phone. Leaving a room, he turns off the light as though I don't exist. I witness this event more than once but doubt its reality: I sit in the dark, my misery throwing itself against the shadows. In darkness I start over, trying to figure it out. By what alchemy does L. complete me when he's so sketchy himself?

How can the two halves of this novel ever be closed or complete? Or the book is a triptych: I follow L. on the left, Margery follows Jesus on the right, and in the center my fear hollows out "an empty space that I can't fill." (That's how Ed describes his death.)

14

Margery needed to talk to everyone now that she was estranged from her life in Lynn.

In late August she traveled with John to take a vow of chastity before Philip, Bishop of Lincoln. The road was flat and straight as the roads of the Fens tend to be; it ran beside a sluggish green canal. Canals and shallow ponds continued the flat plane in stronger greens. The summer's broad emptiness dwarfed the invented world. Margery felt excited, empty handed as a windmill. She wanted Jesus and longed to be rid of sensation.

An old woman nodded in the sun by a tiny mud cottage. At her feet a dog—a bitch for chasing spirits. A rowboat, dainty as a toy, moored to the bank. Margery longed for resolution. The plop of a rising fish, the *creck creck* of a moorhen.

They waited most of September at the Bishop's gate. Then Philip said, "I've long wanted to speak with you." He seemed happy to see Margery, happier to see John. Philip held a yellow apple. Margery asked if, after he had eaten, they could speak for a few hours about Jesus.

Philip lifted his hands and face in wild speculation. "You can talk for two hours about Jesus? I won't be able to eat a thing till I hear what you say!" He concluded the sentence but sustained his gesture like a mannequin, both hands raised towards Margery. Philip had a square Irish face, a beaky nose, and he spoke with such exaggerated courtesy Margery wondered if he was ridiculing her, or the idea of manners.

A sliver of peel wedged itself between Philip's molar and gum. He couldn't get it out with his finger; the tip of his dagger released the coppery taste of blood. John wore a short velvet robe with open sleeves; he sat with his ankles crossed delicately and his enormous chest curved over his lap. Margery told Philip the secrets of the living and dead. "You should write a book," he enthused. He listened with a spellbound smile though Margery could see it was John who enchanted him—John's powerful sweetness and gravity.

John knelt, gazing without reserve into Philip's eyes, and put his hands between Philip's in a vow of chastity. John said, "May her body be as open to Jesus as it was to me."

Another day Margery went to dinner at the Bishop's palace. Her fingertips skimmed the handrail; her jaw dropped in wonder as she floated gently upwards without touching the treads. Philip wore a musty ocelot vest; he distributed thirteen pence and thirteen loaves to thirteen poor men on their grateful knees in a semicircle. Jesus handed Margery some bunched-up paper. She opened it and found only trash inside. He gloated like a tomboy who'd won a bet. Horror of the unexpected amplified her tears. Margery wept so hard that the Bishop's household's foreheads wrinkled in disbelief.

She sat with clerks, priests, and squires, and ate chicken broth thickened with pounded almonds and flavored with cloves, coriander, and thyme; black pudding and sausage; lampreys and herring; meat potages; and tiny local shrimp whose flavor was surprisingly full bodied. From the high table, the Bishop sent her wine and roasted mutton sauced with raisins and nuts and served with quince preserves.

Philip was so sociable that when his face relaxed it grinned. His judgment was based on how much fun he was having because society was falling apart, but his clerks grilled Margery. They were amazed she answered so well. She loved to be examined and ratified.

After dinner Margery said, "I am commanded to tell you to clothe me all in white."

Philip hesitated. "First prove yourself and become recognized."

To prove herself, she told him a story: "A bishop sees a floating bladder; he follows it over hedgerows and fences, through sties and meadows, till he comes to a witch. The bladder stops and sinks to the ground. The bishop says, 'Is this your bladder?' The witch replies, 'Yes.' The bishop says, 'How do you make it float?' The witch says, 'It's easy.' 'Could I do it?' 'Certainly, go ahead.' He tries but nothing happens."

Philip asked, "Why not?"

"That's what the bishop in the story asks. 'Because you have no faith.'"

Philip stared a moment, then laughed and danced a little jig. He decided to send Margery to Lambeth Palace, to Arundel, Archbishop of Canterbury—"And pray him to give me leave to grant your request."

15

Margery and John entered the hall at Lambeth Palace in the afternoon. The walls were painted in blue and gold diamonds and a sideboard stood at the back. Clerks and yeomen swore oaths that tortured Jesus's golden flesh. Margery took sins against language personally.

"Do you know how God was made?" A squire pumped his finger into his fist. "Fucking and shitting!"

Margery said, "You will go straight to hell!" She harangued the crowd with images of ruin and begged Jesus for mercy on their behalf. They gaped at her as though towers were already toppling. A Spanish woman lurched forward; she had black eyebrows and wore heavy silver jewelry. The woman felt sick; a skull jeered its way through her flesh. "I wish you were in Smithfield—and I would bring a bundle of sticks to burn you with!"

Margery stood trembling. Whenever the Spanish woman had a problem she looked for a devil to blame. She singled Margery out and led the mob. (Later she took a turn for the worse and leprosy broke out all over her body. She wanted to hold up a lantern in the darkness to isolate Margery's face.)

Just then the Archbishop sent for Margery. The Spanish woman stretched her arms towards heaven and fell on her knees. The police state was just beginning and she assumed Margery was meeting her doom.

Arundel was a prelate of royal blood. Twelve years earlier, in 1401, he'd rushed an act through Parliament that authorized the burning of heretics. Nine days before the act became law, he burnt a priest from St. Margaret's, Margery's church, for saying good men are holier than angels. Later, in 1410, he burnt Bradly the Tailor, a Lollard who said a spider and a toad are worth more than the consecrated host since they are alive.

Arundel invited Margery to sit in his garden. He had chalky skin and a red nose, the patrician bearing and tight gray ringlets of a schoolmarm.

A bee backed out of a lily trumpet. A turtle walked resolutely across the path, shifting attitudes of attention. Margery started small. She asked Arundel for permission to receive communion every Sunday—unusual at that time but not exceptional. He consented with a nod. His gray eyes drifted, diluted in thick lenses. Thus established, Margery asked him for authority to wear white clothes— to confirm her affair with Jesus. Her voice was a clear bell that broke at the highs with a scratch of emphasis. He approved. Margery exulted; she warned him to restrain his household, especially from swearing oaths on the body of Jesus. Margery talked so fast the Archbishop could hear her gasp between sentences. "You will answer for it, unless you correct them or put them out of your service."

Arundel looked up when he cleaned his lenses. He responded mildly and their conversation continued through the autumn dusk. When his retainers annoyed him with questions asked in weak voices, annihilation woke in his huge distorted eyes and Margery saw the Arundel who burnt heretics. He barked a series of commands; the last—*"Put your heads down!"*—canceled all the others. He told Margery, "Nothing like a little Law to cow the ruffians, my dear!"

The retainers crept away and laid their heads on their folded arms; soon their bodies softened with boredom and they fell asleep on the lawn and the turf seats, alone or draped over each other like hamsters. Arundel sat on his stone throne, his tall hat naked on a cloth next to him, while Margery paced back and forth. Her hands went first, outlining in the dark her entire life up to that moment. They talked till stars appeared above the elms.

16

Margery lost her friends. A community is founded on finitude; there can be no community of immortal beings. Here's a typical story: Jesus sends her to Catherine Hungerford, a respectable lady whose husband died at sea two years before, in 1411. In welcome, Catherine touches her heart with both hands, fingers spread like fans. She feels her mother's voice and gestures in herself as gracefulness.

Eternity is organized as a warm October evening, so it's odd and perhaps beautiful that the lady has a thick fire burning. She has a large supply of wood at hand for processing dyes. Margery takes in the cut of Catherine's sleeve, the length of the hem. Margery makes impossible wishes—for someone's age, money, talent, clothes, eyes—then waits a pressured moment to give the wish time. Finally she states, "Madame, your husband is in purgatory. He will be saved but he will take a long while to get to heaven."

Catherine's husband was a good man and she misses him; she watches her desires yellow into problems and fall from the branch. Why has Margery denied her own husband to pursue the indefinite Jesus with an endless monologue?

Catherine is angry but also worried about Margery. She sends her daughter Jane to Margery's anchorite confessor, asking him to abandon Margery. Jane wears a net of gold mesh through which strands of gold hair gleam. Her cunt lips hang and her swelling hips feel as though they belong to someone else—enormous, round, good to put her hands on. She has her grandmother's figure. The anchorite declines.

Margery confronts Catherine. "Your husband has thirty years in purgatory unless he has better friends on earth. You must pay three or four pounds for him in masses and charity."

Four pounds is a lot of money and thirty years not such a long time. Catherine tells Margery not to visit her again. In Catherine's contempt Margery regains contact with Jesus, but she frets about the heinous Spanish woman at Lambeth Palace. Jesus wants to marry her, Philip and Arundel think she's *exemplary*. Why does the charge of mismanagement slide under her happiness and subvert it?

Jesus perched naked on a banquette, eating a pear tart, rejoicing in bland fragrant sweetness. He offered a slice to Margery, who never refused pastry. He tucked his cock between his legs and wore a flushed, mocking face. He crossed his legs tighter, displaying only sparse brown hair. The ground slid away; Margery's dirty laugh hovered over an empty space because the joke was against her.

Jesus got dressed as a knight. His purple doublet was padded over the chest; he fastened the four-petaled buttons and set a heavy gold belt around his hips. The tension between masculine-feminine and inside-outside pervades all levels of my community. Margery's nose lifted to catch his scent as he passed. "Jesus, did you miss me?" He felt helpless, weak. To regain control he rolled his eyes as though he'd been dragged through the subject a thousand times and sheltered her in his arms in paternal exasperation.

"Ask what you wish. I shall say to you, my own beloved spouse, 'Welcome to me, here to dwell with me and never to depart from me, but ever to dwell with me in joy and bliss.'"

If I say I love you too often, it's partly amazement at the strength of my desire.

Jesus does not miss Margery though he seems to need her. Before storms she feels intolerable expectation.

Confronted by my demands, L. extinguishes all response. His feelings flatten into a wall of mute, introspective despair.

I learn it's exquisite to be fucked by a big cock because it stays pliable till the moment of orgasm. Because of the pleasure I'm beautiful, poised on my fingertips and the balls of my feet like a runner at the starting line.

Jesus kisses her too quickly, jamming his tongue down her throat; he says, "I'm horny."

I perform my story by lip-synching Margery's loud longing but I wonder if that visible self-erasure is just a failure to face L. I want to be a woman and a man penetrating him, his inner walls rolling around me like satin drenched in hot oil, and I want to be the woman and man he continually fucks. I want to be where total freedom is. I push myself under the surface of Margery's story, holding my breath for a happy ending to my own.

In this novel every sentence is a discrete image of promise. A car door slams; I think it must be L.

Margery is traveling.

"Margery, I'd like to send you to Jerusalem and to Rome."

"Jesus, where will I get the money?"

He stammered, "I'll be going too... We'll meet in Jerusalem. I'd like to dress you for the trip." He dropped a stack of coins on the table, enough for a white gown of worsted wool like people wear in heaven, and a veil and wimple. He slid a gold band on her finger and retreated to a three-legged stool to observe the effects of his generosity.

Waving her hand above her head like a flag, Margery laughed with victory. At that time, a visit to Jerusalem guaranteed direct admission to heaven, so what could tear

Margery and Jesus apart? She was intensely relieved and ready for all kinds of action. This trip would be their honeymoon. She was traveling towards the youth of her own body, towards freedom and fame. Her joy welled up, so potent she had to lie down and attend it, dizzy and drunk. Jesus didn't like his life; she would know what to do with his beauty and wealth and in the process make both of them happy.

Margery settled her debts and also John's, as she had agreed to do. She said good-bye to John, who wept bitterly, and to her anchorite confessor, who raised a crooked finger and predicted she would have trouble with her maid but a broken-backed man would escort her wherever she wanted to go—and it did happen that way.

It was early January, 1414. Margery joined a regular party of pilgrims because it was not safe to travel alone. They went to Norwich and then on to Yarmouth. The clouds were only slightly lighter and larger than the boulders they resembled and they rumbled across the sky. The pilgrims booked passage across the North Sea. Africans made up a quarter of the crew. Vs of pelicans slid through the air. The group planned to go overland to Venice, from there sail to Jerusalem and back again, and then head south to Rome. Tours to the Holy Land were well organized. The ship docked next day in a town called Zierikzee, in Zealand.

PART TWO
The Jerusalem Journey

Thou hast gouyn me drynkyn ful many tymes wyth teerys of thyn eye.

17

Margery and the other pilgrims sat down to dinner in a tavern so bright and noisy it revolved on itself like a gyroscope. Blasts of icy air interrupted the stifling heat. The pilgrims were in high spirits, looking forward to the trip. An old woman took their order; she acted slow because she had huge deaf ears. The pilgrims laughed while a little boy stared at them.

Margery's maid was shy and ambitious; she hung back, laughing with the rest. The maid was so thin her hip bones stuck out like handle bars: she felt ideal and aerated. She needed privacy and scrutinized people's expressions as they approached.

A priest made a quick blessing over beans and vegetable soup served by the grandmother. She had been a woman of great sophistication. When she fucked a man, she would elevate one of her legs vertically. A lamp full of oil, wick burning, was set on her foot, and while he rammed her she kept the flame steady.

They all drew their knives and began eating. Margery started to whimper; her ovaries were sponges that soaked up energy from people and situations. The pilgrims were concerned. A widow asked, "Don't you like our company?" She remembered the arrogant young woman Margery had been.

Margery wore the open eyes of blunt wonder: Jesus was exploding her social circle. "I welcome the twelve apostles, the holy virgins, martyrs—Jesus sleeps in my bed, he calls me his dear darling!"

The pilgrims were stunned. The priest said, "Be quiet, Margery. Jesus died long ago." Wine had given him the sensation of emptiness.

Margery couldn't stop talking: she sought recognition in the theater of her voice. *"I cry you mercy, Ihesu, for al the pepil in this world, that you make ther sinnys to me."* Her love for Jesus isolated her so she pursued any reaction to it—hostility or praise. She had a sore throat and enjoyed the rawness as if heat were biting her. "Jesus sits on a red cushion. I could never requite his love though I were slain a thousand—"

The priest cried, "I hope the devil's death overtakes you soon and quickly!"

"I have as great a reason to speak of Jesus here as in England." She felt valid when she said his name.

The pilgrims threw up their hands. Her white clothes were a continual affront. If she was not Jesus's bride, her hypocrisy dismantled the entire world; if she *was* supernatural, she attracted the extreme: pestilence and hunger, steeples toppling, trees ripped out of the earth. "You cannot go any farther with us and we intend to keep your maid." The young woman remained silent.

Next morning one of the pilgrims advised Margery to find the others and behave meekly. They took her with them, following the Rhine valley across Europe, but they cut her white gown so short it hung only a little below her knees, made her wear a white canvas apron like a fool, and sat her at the bottom of the table, below everyone.

In Constance, the pilgrims washed their hands of her. They returned her money, about twenty pounds—sixteen pounds were wrongfully withheld—and they kept her maid, who had promised never to abandon her.

18

In the square in Constance an old man from Devonshire approached Margery with a grin. "Will you ask me to be your guide?"

She returned his smile. "What is your name?"

"My name is Willyam Wever." He had a white beard and heavy gray pouches under muddy hazel eyes. His coat was thick as a board. Margery's expression faltered as she realized he always smiled.

She said good-bye to the pilgrims who had abandoned her and set off into the Alps with a long face; she didn't know her guide and he didn't know Italian. Murder, violation, nightfall, strange men: her chance to live forever heightened her fear of death. They both felt anxious. Willyam Wever's persistent grin was a structural cruelty, like the genial expression a frog must wear even as it disappears down the gullet of a snake. Between smiles he said, "You'll be taken from me—you'll be raped—they'll beat me up—steal my coat—"

It was mid-February. Willyam wound his tippet around his neck and sheltered his hands in his armpits; his empty sleeves swung woodenly. Larch and fir grew below snowy peaks. The travelers were flushed with expanding harmonies of wind, space, drizzle, clouds, and thick greens; her words were lost in the wind; snipes zigzagged crying *chip-per, chip-per.* The road skirted the steepest rocks and in places was hewn out of them. Margery climbed with amazing stamina; Willyam smiled and wheezed. The bottom of his right foot was so sore he cringed when he stepped. They ate boar sausage and stuffed gooseneck. She was traveling; every bowel movement was a triumph. Watermills turned above foaming rivers.

They climbed up to Resia and over the pass. Snow lay thick and abundant, massed on branches, glittering wealth that could not be acquired. Wolves had crossed leaving delicate prints. Stars swarmed upwards, then the moon held the white peaks in a trance. Pale mountains grew smaller in the radiant sunrise. Melting snow water coursed downhill in rills that wagon wheels pressed in the mud. The foothills were covered by sloping vineyards and dotted by whitewashed houses. Almond trees bloomed palest pink. Cowherds tended white cattle splattered with black spots and gave the travelers food and drink; their wives put Margery in their own beds.

A horse was hag-ridden. Its owners filled a bottle with its urine, stopped it with a cork, and buried it: the witch could not piss and died in agony. The air hummed with flies when the travelers approached the cattle—rich odors of dung and hay. They heard an ouzel's ringing *tew tew tew;* the peasants cupped their ears. Farmers tilled their small fields to the limit. Women carded and combed, clouted and washed, and peeled rushes as in Lynn. One woman became a man when he jumped over an irrigation ditch and his cunt dropped inside out: gender is the extent we go to in order to be loved. His mittens were made of rags.

Pastures sloped down to a rich valley divided into square farms, fields of rye grass for winter forage, and silvery olive orchards where blue tits sang *tsee-tsee-tsu-tsuhuhuhu.* In Bolzano, women trading in silk and leather in the square discussed Margery and Willyam as they arrived. Later, Margery woke feeling her heart skip a beat, another, another, as though it fell down stairs and she—laughing in surprise—scrambled after it.

When the pilgrims arrived in Bolzano, they were amazed to find Margery there and decided the spiritual advantage of readmitting her to their party might extend to speed and safety on the highway.

Margery had been traveling for two months and she itched with desire. Her scalp itched and her skin crawled. All movement in time and space led to orgasm. When she arrived in Venice with the pilgrims there was still plenty of rain and cold, but she grasped the city's beauty in the form of Jesus: gold light exulting over the big squares and on the water, the muddy narrow alleys, the clink of a courtyard fountain, always the layering of cool air over hot air, the yammering cats.

L. returns from the street with pastry for breakfast. From bed, I hear clanks, a faucet's hiss, fat spitting. We eat in harsh tremulous silence, caffeine tension riding above the emptied-out clarity of sex in the morning.

I follow L. He knows how to climb through narrow shafts of the Plaza Hotel to the roof. We share an intense visual life—all Central Park below us. Our best days are spent with attention turned outwards. He runs his tongue across the wind on his lips. His features are tense with perfection; they create the sensation of beauty as focus. We stroll around Boston, New York, San Francisco, Charleston, Florence, Sienna, Compostela, and Lisbon. I look for glimpses of him in other men through the lens of my attraction, then glimpses of his spirit in everything the world designs.

Very moody days in Venice, somewhat empty. Dark churches. It's exhausting to trail after him and not talk about us, but my fatigue doesn't count even to myself. I stop and he continues speeding around a corner. A moment of elation rises in space above the reflection of that space. Then I'm stymied—I'm nowhere. At the hotel we don't mention the hours apart. He strokes my ass—it's his faithful dog basking in attention that seems honest because absent-minded. Later, he brings oranges to bed and feeds me sections.

Lunch at the market, roast chicken, book box in antique store, wall paintings of fruit trees. I spend too much trying to keep up. I fret passionately: What should I own?

We look at some green velvet stamped with gold. I complain, "It's too fragile—it's what rich people would buy."

"Do you mean to say, people rich with a highly developed sense of aesthetics?"

Walking back slowly, we stop to consider a play of features, a hat, a dish, winter light skittering on the feathery needles of a hemlock; for a moment we are only that awareness. The image holds and displays the promise of the wide world, then we walk on with a pang of regret.

Venice grew crowded as spring progressed. At dusk the population spilled into the streets and piazzas, sweetly murmurous, still dazed from the light.

Margery's maid prepared the company's food and washed their clothes; she washed dishes and clothes, her submerged hands squeezing out dirt, but she would not attend Margery or explain why she had abandoned her.

19

Pilgrims bought tours of the Holy Lands from ship captains stationed in Venice who negotiated package deals with the Saracens. The galleys usually left Venice in spring or early summer.

Margery's company arranged for a ship at the beginning of May; they bought provisions, wine and bedding, but only for themselves. Margery intended to sail with them but Jesus assigned her to a many-oared Venetian galley. Seeing this, the pilgrims lost faith in their own ship. They switched at the last minute, taking a financial loss; furious, they lugged their bedding in bales crisscrossed with rope.

The galley smelled like tar and resin. The sea was intense, abstract. Brutal oarsmen. A priest stole a sheet. Margery's berth was a rectangle chalked on the boards long enough to lie down in. She woke in the noisy crowded hold with a jolt of longing so vibrant she thought she was falling. She slid her hand between her legs and found it wet there. Her love was mixed with a desire to arrive and succeed. They sailed south along the Dalmatian coast, then east through the Greek islands. Piss, rancid meat, moldy cloth, farts. The sailors' bare feet slapped the wooden deck. A deep wind rose in the sky of her hearing. The voyage lasted thirty days. The pilgrims tormented her. "I pray you, sirs, be in charity with me, for I am in charity with you, and forgive me if I have amazed you along the way."

She was riding a donkey across blighted land when she glimpsed Jerusalem, a fantastic jewel with thick walls, towers and ramparts, buildings stacked like crystals, gold onion domes weightless above the sum total of terrestrial experience, the beautiful slow time that Jesus owned. I cross intercosmic distance to embrace L. I would not cling to existence if I believed in it more. Heaven is belief in the future, endless meaning, endless narration. Two blond Germans kept Margery upright. They heard the ringing *kata*,

kata, kata of sandgrouse but the sky was too bright to see them overhead. Intimate touch made a promise of immortality. "So thanks, Jesus, and let me see the city of heaven as well. To live forever is to live in the future."

Jesus dropped into Margery's ear and cried, "You will!"

Surprise almost knocked her to the ground. "Sirs, I beg you, don't be amazed though I weep bitterly." The Germans didn't speak English.

The heat was a demand but each cool breeze was heavier fulfillment. This time the sun sank in front of the mountain. Dusk fell in an instant, the cloth backdrop, the palms. Shadows quickly climbed bare slopes.

The Latin kings of Jerusalem built the Church of the Holy Sepulchre three hundred years before. Saracens collected entrance fees and admitted the group at evensong, to remain till evensong next day. Inside, friars led the pilgrims to places where Jesus suffered. They all carried wax candles. At Calvary, a rocky hill fourteen feet high, a turbulence grew in Margery: she was ashamed; she wrestled with her body, holding it in as long as she could; she flung her arms apart and screamed, quick and extended as an insect shedding its shell. The pilgrims stared in horror. Some said it was an illness or that she drank too much wine; some wished her at sea in a bottomless boat.

Jesus hung before her in his manhood, his beauty tense as glass, his milky skin more full of holes than a dovecote, his long white feet nailed to the hard wood, blood gushing from every limb, the grisly wound beneath the tiny pink nipple—

When they came to the grave where Jesus was buried, *fel sche down wyth hir wax candel* (as Margery wrote), palms pressed against her breast, sweat streaming in icy rills. Two angels held her shoulders and a third lifted a tear from her cheek onto its thumbnail where it glistened in the brown-velvet shadows. The angel wore a white deacon's robe. It deported itself like a maître d' presenting rare brandy. Gazing at the tear with a hollow expression, Jesus felt the heat and weight of his cock snake across his thigh. He steadied the angel's hand, lapped up the tear with his pointed tongue, and then it was the angel's turn to steady Jesus: his legs trembled, he convulsed with pleasure as he clenched against it, an underwater scream. He slid to the side, gritting his teeth and groaning. His fine skin became invulnerable, the bright armor of the intoxicated. The angels' inky wings were a melancholy flourish.

Margery and Jesus were reunited. "Don't be ashamed to weep for Jesus... Mary Magdalene wasn't ashamed." Mary said this in a breathy whisper and wavered in mild pervasive distortion when Margery visited her grave; she cupped Margery's breasts in her hands. She viewed Margery's nipples as an opportunity to multiply flavor, skin tasting honey or sugar. Margery was too surprised to move and wondered what had chipped and dirtied Mary's nails. Mary was naked beneath the thin chemise of a bathhouse attendant; a sheer scarf loosely hooked to her crown flowed downwards with her golden hair. "St. Stephen wore green tippets...when we stoned him..."

20

The pilgrims would not let Margery go to the River Jordan. Jesus said, "We'll go whether they like it or not."

Margery and Jesus followed them through a wilderness of thorns. The ground burned Margery's feet and the distant rim didn't even ripple. Hermits wearing cloth of thorn and camel hair ate locusts and sat grimacing on anthills as though easing into too-hot tubs. Vultures croaked and whistled, wings raised in pious attitudes. An oasis held a lake so clear it didn't seem to exist; it made her want to laugh, weightless. She was so thirsty her tongue reached the water before her lips.

The road ran straight towards the sky, permanent. Margery and Jesus walked along the ridge, their long shadows bowing into the valley, curvatures of agreement. A kite sailed in buoyant flight, extended wings and forked tail in sharp silhouette. Margery had confidence in her body and the naked Jesus was an athlete; when he'd sprained his ankle he was mad at the ankle, not at himself. The muddy river wound between steep banks. The Saracens forbade anyone to dive under water or swim across to gather willows. Pilgrims often drowned; a paralysis came over them even though Jesus was a strong swimmer.

"Did you miss me, Jesus?" Her question twisted him beyond endurance like the fibers of a rope. It had taken days to unwind; now he was cold and aloof again. Just the tip of his lanky cock was interested in Margery. He jogged ahead up the gray path on his way to Rome. Soft puffs hovered above his footprints. Margery held her arms out as though to touch him through the air. She thought they would always be together. She called but he didn't look back.

The friars welcomed Margery and sold her the hair and bones of saints, a kind of pornography in that even fragments of the aroused body have value. Margery spent so much money that the friars wanted her to remain with them. The Saracens who organized the tour also admired her zeal and tears. Everyone liked Margery except her own countrymen, who felt trapped in the sound of her voice.

The pilgrims backtracked from Jerusalem to Ramleh and returned to their ship. Many fell ill, vomiting and feverish; Margery heard their groans and violent coughs on deck and then their horrible cries below where they fucked while the ship endlessly pitched. Fear made them clumsy. Margery stumbled on the chief mate and her maid in a hidden corner of the deck: he was joyously stroking the girl's small breasts, sending shock waves through her entire body. Her nipples grew rigid as marbles. He was thirty years old; her skin was so soft he started to purr. He saw the maid as a symbol of abundance, a luck he couldn't encompass because it included his own life. She thought, "Now I know I have something men want." She wasn't sure if she was still a virgin, which line had to be crossed.

21

They docked in Venice on July 18. The round-trip had taken eleven weeks. The pilgrims abandoned Margery again and set out for Rome. In the Piazza San Marco a beggar with a hump caught her eye. His coat was of carry-marry cloth and he was about fifty. She cried, "What's wrong with your back?"

"Broken in an illness." That was hard to imagine. Richard was from Ireland. A scab grew in the middle of his forehead. He was twisted over; gray hair poked through the holes in his hood; his shoes were thickly cobbled though his grimy toes appeared when he walked.

"Richard, guide me to Rome."

Panic yanked him backwards. "Your countrymen abandoned you. They have bows and arrows to defend themselves—I have nothing but patches. My enemies will rob me and rape you."

"I will pay you two nobles and Jesus will provide."

Richard wrapped himself in a winnowing sheet to keep out the weather. They rode south to Pesaro, then turned inland into the Apennines. A waterfall fell white on brown rocks below; they couldn't hear it thunder till they passed by. In Richard, Margery met her match at nonstop talking. She pissed in silence behind an oleander, a puddle frothing on the hard dirt. At night a steady wind pushed the campfire's flame and the shifting branches above looked like snowflakes rising. The travelers saw their shadows by moonlight and Margery could read the inscription on the ring Jesus had given her, JESUS IS MY LOVER.

Margery pretended to sleep, listening in horror while Richard talked to their fire. The flame conveyed a sense of continuous beginning; he told it that his platoon fucked a whore in France with *sweet* and *sour* tattooed on her breasts—the whore fainted and he tucked her in.

He told his hand that once he had talked to a tree, that a tree is a bush with a hard-on. Margery couldn't figure out where he got the bottles of wine but she could see from his drunken gestures that he thought he was in tune with the universe. He raised his arms and face above his crooked frame, fingers high in the air, and shrugged with good-natured exasperation. He asked them all—fire, hand, tree—what Margery was going to put him through next day.

Before dawn Richard vomited on his hands and knees, shouting with each burst, "Look out, she's ready to blow!"

Richard led Margery to Assisi, a walled city perched on a little mountain, and to the church where Mary's kerchief was exhibited. Lamas Day, August 1, was the date of the Portiuncula indulgence, an important pardon with plenary remission.

A lady had traveled to Assisi to obtain pardon. Her name was Dame Margaret Florentyne and she came from Rome with other ladies and Knights of Rhodes. Richard asked Margaret in Italian if they could join her party and then continued in English, "Either the tide is going in or going out." Margaret nodded as if she understood. Dame Margaret experienced herself as discrete lake waves, small encouragements from a larger source, internalized into a lifelong refrain. She was the mirror of fifteenth-century beauty: straight nose, gray eyes, little pink mouth, and skin so smooth it blurred. It was an honor for her to protect a holy woman; she admired Margery's tears and couldn't understand a word of her story.

Margaret traveled on pillows in an open horse litter faced in leather on which her coat of arms was stamped in gold.

The skin's dry heat and the dry grass scent. At night, a woodlark. Richard sang,

> *The moon does always piss*
> *When she is pale,*
> *When red, she farts, when white,*
> *She wipes her tail.*

It hurts me to see L. sleep, his long head half-supported by his jacket hanging next to the window; in the crowded coach he is isolated by my desire. We both had our first orgasms when we were about eleven—with a sense of isolation and estrangement from our bodies. L.'s ex died of AIDS. They'd had some unsafe sex. Is that how it will go?—Will sickness weaken L. till he accepts my love?

Nothing can be seen outside except the occasional fog-held glow of a streetlight that burns through our intense reflections: a couple chats, a woman does a cross-word puzzle, a man reads a paper. The women wear stylish glasses. Bright dots jump off jewels and wristwatches. The world that appears has the look of the world of appearance.

L.'s eyelashes flutter; he whispers "Bob the Mo-ronist," and I grin moronically. I can orient myself only with an abridged self-knowledge; I can fulfill myself only by revealing our hidden parts. I reiterate the six hairs on his chest, the brown patch above his cock, and the few curls around his asshole. The air is heavy despite the no-smoking sign. A "scroll of parchment" is pinned to the wall above L.'s head: the word *Roma* on a ribbon unfurling above medieval towns with towers and ships in a river. Even asleep, L.'s body promises travel.

I keep dropping off. My legs fall against his legs unconsciously and with painful readiness. I'm reluctant to lose control of my limbs in a crowded compartment. Emptiness wants me to yield, order wants me to stay awake.

22

Rome was not Venice; it was rough, plague ridden, almost derelict. Mountains of decaying refuse poisoned the water. Since early August, it had been revolting from the King of Naples's government. The urine-discolored streets were nothing but potholes littered with garbage, pariah dogs, and beggars and whores of all sexes drawn helplessly from the overtaxed surrounding farms and towns—the whole covered by fat flies that rose snarling in unison. Dead horses, donkeys, and children were thrown into vacant houses on ruined streets and left for rats and dogs because it was easier than dragging the corpses out-side the city gates. Even buzzards found their way into these charnel houses. For a moment Margery wondered if it was snowing: ashes floated everywhere. The chief industry consisted in burning the marble of classical Rome to produce lye.

The pilgrims were already there; Margery joined them at the Hospital of St. Thomas of Canterbury, the hostel for English pilgrims in the Via Monserrato.

She was given a room with shutterless windows that opened onto a back garden. A neighbor's jasmine encumbered the hot breeze. An arbor covered half the yard; broad leaves caught the shadows of broad leaves above, their mass suggested by tones of light, the green grapes immature. The old garden wall had the wisdom to be stupid, its mortar spongy, its mass suggested by edges.

Margery exulted in lucidity as though her mind were erect. She untied Jesus's codpiece. Jesus gravely lifted each leg so she could peel his hose off; he was starting to enjoy the attention. Margery felt the charm of taming a skittish animal, shy with its emotions, then completely present. Mullions' dull shadows on the whitewashed wall, mosquitoes adrift in the corners of the ceiling, chatter of unseen birds and the monotonous scales of someone's flute. Through the leaves the sky was an afterthought.

He exhaled loudly; she could hear the tension leaving him. His bony face softened, disheveled and staring. Pre-come gathered in a sticky puddle below his navel; he kept losing his erection. She drew her forearm across her brow but her arm was as sweaty as her face. Her outer lips were moist and slightly parted, swelling in helpless lechery. She felt his breath on her curls and clit, his saliva left a surprising coolness on her ass and thigh.

Jesus the athlete moved with her easily. He aroused her with his long burrowing tongue. He pulled her hair aside and drew her clit into his mouth. "It's too much." She squirmed away from the intensity. He rolled it on his tongue till he felt it rise. Margery's moan was low and fluty, faint and continuous; the folds of her cunt slid against each other and her pinched nipples made her hips tip forwards. She rejoiced in the absence of fear. He opened his pores to let sweat pass through; a trickle rolled down his chest and dropped onto her belly. A low vibration commenced as her body generated pleasure. He watched her womb roil the surface of her stomach and he lapped up his accomplishments.

Margery's senses were entirely awake in lush satisfaction, a subtle fire in the darkness of a sleeping world though daylight fell plainly in their room. Her hands roamed across his skin; he pulled back; she was groaning; her foaming juice equaled a lucent sweetness. Pleasure burned through all expression allowing a different truth to appear, their faces bare as china dolls. Every second they thought, *This could be it*; he did not make a sound except one note as a deep quaver swept through his ass and balls and traveled the length of his cock. They held absolutely still at the first spurt. The strongest pleasure that can exist occurred in Jesus's cock: ecstasy was not parsed out in spasms; for all time sperm spills steadily down the shaft.

Satisfied desire set her in a world where satisfied desire was the only possibility. Being with Jesus was like breathing underwater or flying: the granting of a childhood wish for ease in a different medium. She lay facing him, her red hair fanned out behind. Arms and legs draped over each other, lips touched in ardent peace. Margery adjusted so they breathed together. Inside the moment she held him forever, at rest and in continuous flight.

Around the rustic bed stood angels in court dress, their faces aware as lightning. Their baggy sleeves were drawn at the wrist and they echoed Margery and Jesus, passing around the jubilant life. Her body smelled like his. She thought that confirmed an undecaying union. She heard neighbors' shutters bang, the rap of unripe figs dropping on the garden flags, and she watched the light soften into long afternoon while Jesus slept. Wings surrounded them. She felt unbelievably lucky.

The first cool breeze, Jesus said, "The more men want you, the better I dress you." He promised Margery a white cotton mantle and veil. She drew close and sought eye contact; he had a persistent cough she wanted to nurse. He was moved by her devotion but also bewildered and hemmed in. He said with a cough, "I don't have a cough." Then, "Except when I'm with you." He cocked his pointed face as though viewing her from afar.

He stood up and she followed him into the dusty garden. "If it were possible I would weep with you." He hesitated, dazzled; he smelled sage. With his feet turned out and his knock-knees and his broad hips tipped forwards and his pointed nose in the air, Margery observed with tender hilarity that her lover looked like an ostrich.

Random fires on the black hills. Clumsy beige moths that crumbled into dry smudges when she touched them. Above, inky clouds lifted in the twilight: it was a longing within her. She never forgot that night. She said, "Jesus, grant me a well of tears through which to receive your body."

23

An English priest, one of the pilgrims, was attracted to Margery. He was a thin man in his early twenties with wiry black hair. Black curls were sprouting on his butt; he watched them grow with a puzzled expression. He needed to be vindicated. He recognized in Margery the fireworks he wished to ignite in himself, as though unfettered passion were available to everyone, and he locked her in a fixed, painstaking squint. He did not dispute that she had supernatural gifts—but were they malevolent?

The sun was so bright the shadows of trees seemed to ride on water instead of white dirt. Margery needed support in Rome. She took her broken-backed man to Wenslawe, the priest at St. John Lateran, who asked in German, "Are you the woman who speaks with Jesus?" She was becoming famous.

Wenslawe understood no English so they spoke through Richard. The priest was learned and beloved; he held one of the richest offices in Rome—jasper, malachite, onyx, opal, lapis, and alabaster. He was blond, solemn, his face square as a shoebox. Wenslawe did not have much Promethean fire. Inside himself he was always raising his hand to his forehead, a flighty, hapless gesture at odds with his looks. Margery asked him to pray to understand her English and she would also pray for understanding.

The English priest spread rumors about Margery because her white clothes turned the earth of his heart upside down. His wish to become Margery made him hostile, frightening. He was so critical that people began to justify their existence before they met his ferreting eyes. Margery undressed with her back to the window; she felt observed all the time. He watched her narrowly and said, "You make me sick." In fact, he was always feeling for the onset of disease. He called Margery *hypocrite* and *whore* till the pilgrims refused to eat with her and she was thrown out of the Hospital of St. Thomas.

Margery needed allies. She returned to Wenslawe to test the effect of their prayers. She needed to talk quickly in a clear voice to build a constituency of belief. The German understood her English and she told him her story from childhood to that hour. "Last night the holy virgins decorated my bed with flowers and spices—Jesus slept there—" Her tears made her more intelligible to herself—grueling nausea and self-disgust—but that idea is too far ahead. Wenslawe thought an evil spirit had seized her but her frantic hands looked more like they were trying to seize.

Wenslawe began to have misgivings so Margery confronted him with the failings of his own life: He'd made up lies about himself. He wanted to be more aggressive, more sure. His mother had died on Saturday and he acted as though it hadn't happened. He didn't want other people to see his sadness. She'd had a disease that glued her eyes shut. She'd worn big hats. He'd admired her for wanting to be different. She'd made a statement.

The priest felt caught in a dream whose parts were not disjunct but overrelated. He went to mass and wept so deeply his tears wet his vestments and the ornaments of the altar.

So this good man was not embarrassed to side with Margery against her countrymen. He ordered the Grey Friars to take her in and he instructed her to wear black again for her own safety. Wenslawe was her first conquest in Rome: the Romans loved him even more and loved Margery too; they invited her to dinner.

24

On November 9, 1414, God said to Margery, "Daughter, I'm glad, especially because you love the manhood of my son." These words unrolled from his parted lips on gold ribbon. Margery ascended on the beam of her upturned gaze.

Margery had never seen God before. He resembled Jesus, but his blue eyes were faded and a wreath of silvery olive leaves crowned thinning blond hair. He was comfortable only with servants; he chatted with his wine steward, the servitors, the gardener, the musicians. When Margery asked what she should call him, God became silent, gazing with the family's dazzled expression into the branches of an old oak. Was he trying to remember? Although he had created himself out of shadowy rage, he seemed mild and dry as a country vicar. He said, "I will marry you and show you my secrets so you can live with me forever."

Margery had not founded an order like St. Bridget or promoted church reform like St. Catherine. She looked for glimpses of Jesus in handsome blonds on the streets of Rome. She felt humid, tense misery when she saw beautiful men in the tumultuous streets. Was it surprising that she couldn't answer Jesus's father? The one whose manhood she desired said, "What do you say to my father, Margery? Are you pleased?" She covered her face and wept.

Margery's red hair fell uncovered, a loose pillow, virginal. She wore a purple-velvet mantle banded in gold over a gown of white silk stamped with gold fleur-de-lis. Her huge bag sleeves were trimmed with strips of dagged baby-blue silk. Jesus spoke for her. "Excuse her, she is abashed and can't answer."

The father was loving but unsteady, an apparition that remained. He took Margery by the hand before Jesus, the Ghost, Mary, the twelve apostles, St. Katherine, St. Margaret, *& many other seyntys & awngelys*, as Margery wrote, whose wings were pale ocher blending into pale Venetian red with spidery feathers at the joint. St. Margaret wore red silk brocade from Lucca on which firebirds rose in fastidious elaboration. She said to St. Katherine, "Would you move over a little?" Katherine could only have an orgasm when she was completely passive; she wore a violet gown of chatoyant silk furred with marten; she stepped closer to St. Clare, who wore a nun's habit.

Angels lifted Margery's train. The father said, "I take you, Margery, for my wedded wife, for fairer, for fouler, for righter, for poorer. Never was a child so kind to its mother as I will be to you." He dropped gold and silver coins in the book.

Margery made sucking sounds, trying to suppress her tears. She felt more like a human spy than a bride. The father, Mary, and Jesus were reversible; they juggled amongst themselves the conditions that defined Margery: daughter, wife, mother, her need for money, her mortality, her desire. Mary was a fractured silence, unfolding veils of cool spectral vapor. She smiled brightly to reassure the newly-weds; they leaned towards her. "...an orchestra played to drown her cries...broke all her teeth..." Margery couldn't tell if Mary remembered her. The gods were indifferent to events; a disaster that pulled Margery's body inside out like a dirty sock would have sedated Mary.

"Margery, if you wore a coat of mail, or a hair shirt, or fasted on bread and water, you would not please me so much as when you are *silent* and allow me to speak." God was the grandest religious leader to ask Margery to be quiet.

25

They are eating the Roman wedding supper *al fresco* at a long table laid with a damask cloth. God retires, content in a void. His pomeranians wander freely among the dishes. It's almost later but not quite. The autumn sun comes round and canaries exult in their cages. A citizen of actual paradise preens itself, wings surrounding its torso in place of shoulders and arms: gold and pale Venetian red. Red geraniums and oleanders grow in terra-cotta pots and a square cement fountain glugs periodically. Jesus picks up where his father left off, speaking to everyone but most directly to Margery. "There's more merit in one year in your mind than a hundred praying with your mouth. You will not believe me." He means, longing and weeping are the best love.

Margery considers her love; she could live on his scent, rosy, musty. Flames like human tongues start shifting in her breast—even in winter she will feel hot.

"I take you by the hand because my wife should be on homely terms with her husband. I lie in your bed. You desire to see me; you boldly take me as your wedded husband, your dear darling, for I want to be loved as a son is loved by his mother, and I want you to love me, daughter, as a wife loves her husband."

Now she's wedded to Jesus, but father and son decline to remember which is which. Bellows blow in Margery's ears: it's the sound of the Ghost. Jesus turns it into the tremolo of a dove and then, lighter and shriller, a redbreast's call. It sings in her right ear. She sees she is standing on tiptoe.

Jesus rises and touches Margery's face, darkly romantic. "Take me in your arms and kiss my lips, my head, my feet as sweetly as you wish." Reeling with sweetness, she enters myth. At last her desire organizes the universe. Her conquest of priests and bishops brings fame and power, her marriage to Jesus brings safety and pleasure.

"Even when I stand here and say you can never come to heaven, never see my face, tell me you will never abandon me though you lie in a lake of fire. If you can't exist without loving me, then I am all you have." They kiss over the bride cakes but his eyes are red and swollen and his lips are giving way. His voice quavers as he says, "Margery, make yourself destitute."

Margery followed his command without knowing how to interpret it. He seemed to withdraw in the midst of his marriage vow. She handed out her own money and then money borrowed from Richard. The broken-backed man jumped up and down, raising dust in the street. He was so angry his eyes turned back in his head and for a moment the world was distorted.

A Victorian etching of a sarcophagus in a crypt. On the back of the postcard, L. had copied out these lines by Denton Welch: I saw all this, and Ray's jaw had fallen open, as the jaws of all corpses in schoolboys' books are fallen open. His mouth gaped so that I could see the place where his wisdom teeth had begun to sprout. And his dead tongue was stiff as the metal clapper of a bell and the purple-brown color of burnt iron. "Everything spoilt and wasted," I thought.

This novel records my breakdown; conventional narrative is preserved but the interest lies elsewhere. Like L., Jesus must be real but must also represent a crisis. After Margery gave every penny away, she sat in the rear of Marcellis's church and reminded herself, To Jesus, isn't everyone dependent and voiceless? He complains that his father makes a blind spot of his loved ones, withdraws from a demand, inflicts pain casually, but he duplicates these traits. Discrete rays falling from the lantern windows give shape to my love for L.

26

Jesus and Mary squatted, making little cries, then looked curiously at each other's shit.

Later they sat on a marble bench in the yard outside St. John Lateran. Mary wore a white mantle and robe. The English priest grabbed her white collar. "You wolf, what is this cloth you wear?"

Mary looked happily into his face. Swifts gliding by on stiff wings shrieked, "Wool, sir."

"Now I know you have a devil because I hear him speak."

"Ah, good sir," she laughed, "drive him away, drive him away." Her laughter touched an exposed nerve; the priest lurched back and retreated in confusion.

A light drizzle darkened the flagstones except for a dry gray rectangle under their bench. Contorted roots of umbrella pines had gripped and dislodged some of the stones. Jesus could not define himself through Mary. She caressed the folds of his mantle as though they were membranes. She whispered, "I see pale angels round about you." She felt the thick surge that lifts us towards a person we love. He looked up. The angels were primitive, like golden orchids.

Jesus felt muddled, a fog of sadness closing in. He depended on Margery for motivation but a cold bar plunged through his heart when she asked, Did you miss me? Their time together was more definitive for him since he had much more to define. Their sex was satisfying but he was undermined by the terror of the incomplete: If her cheekbones were higher or personality cooler would their union be more compelling? Safety meant being recognized without returning recognition. That is, everyone was his slave. As though to confirm this, Jesus asked his own mother to beg for Margery's food and wine.

So that night Mary went to a feast with important people—she was disguised but visible. It was not unusual for these banquets to include a pauper who was holy, even divine. She sat at the high table next to Wenslawe, the priest from St. John Lateran. He was like a child, wide eyed with surprise. He ate with his head lowered, then pressed a gold coin in her palm and whispered, "If I have to die, return me as a stylish woman's elaborate earring."

I feel close to Wenslawe and I make Jesus into my own god whose beauty is a lens—intenser light, clearer colors—like sight in heaven. Absolute Good is casting shadows, and when I pull out I am awed that he is stretched wide open and I catch a whiff as sweetly fetid and timeless as any New York sewer.

When I began *Margery*, I took Flaubert's "The Legend of St. Julian Hospitaler" as a model, a moral and supernatural tale by a writer whose entire faith was in writing, as though telling a story perfectly were the same as obtaining forgiveness for existing. I am drawn to modernism but my faith is impure. I am no more the solitary author of this book than I alone invent the fiction of my life. As I write, I read my experience as well as Margery's. Is that appropriation?—that I am also the reader, oscillating in a nowhere between what I invent and what changes me?

When I was a child, belief attracted and repelled me, especially beliefs of Christian friends. Eating the body, drinking blood. Sexual sins whispered into hidden ears. The whacked-out saints, their fragmented corpses. Jesus nursing and the glorious fleshy ham.

There wasn't enough faith to go around. My god inclined towards a darkness which was not interested in my belief or my sins and which continues to be none of my business. Where are the Jewish martyrs, the seven million who return as documentaries? I was raised in a kosher home in the huge Jewish community in Cleveland but I didn't learn of the camps till I saw them on TV in Los Angeles and *then* my mother volunteered with neutral excitement that we'd lost relatives, as though relating us to TV rather than to history. Did she want to protect me from the abnormality of our recent past? Or maybe everyone talked and I wasn't *listening?*

Later I read some mystics and wanted to join a monastery. Illuminating holy books was a career that suited my temperament and passage to this magical universe was simply belief in it.

Jesus and Margery act out my love. Is that a problem? Every star in every galaxy spurts in joyful public salute to my orgasms with L. But I look for the Jew from

Cleveland and he confuses me. A photo from 1988: L.'s sisters, their mates, L., and myself on a wooden bench in L.'s family's compound in the Adirondacks. I am jolted to see five sleek WASPs smiling into the camera and a visitor from an alternative universe—pallid, averted, big headed, un-American. I recognize my isolation, a mix of longing and hostility.

Margery held a mistaken belief in the value of her experience. A tradition I *can* claim as my own links me to her—of farce and uncertainty, the broad comedy of terror, the fable a community of doubt tells itself: "The Pardoner's Tale," the *Talmud*, *The Ship of Fools*, Kafka's slapstick, Freud's case histories, the sarcasm of Marx, Brecht, Fassbinder—

I'm in a wooden tub. Face slack, thoughtless, half submerged, neck severed, trunk and limbs hacked apart and soaking in rotting blood and gore. That seems appropriate, a feeling of accuracy and fulfillment overrides the horror of having been murdered in some derelict industrial subbasement. Poignancy in the disheveled air. The whole atmosphere lives with joyous expectation of a visit from L., who wears a black cape in the dream.

27

Margery went out to beg from the Romans. A woman's body blocked traffic, legs thrown apart, head cocked against a stucco wall where she had died. A naked baby howled on his back and a three-legged nursing stool lay toppled beside him. Margery watched fleas jump off the mother's cooling body; a dead flea jumped back to life when Margery touched it. The screaming baby waved his arms and legs in all directions and Margery felt her breasts swell. The baby was hot, sticky, and sour; he bucked and squealed like a little pig. Margery could hardly hold him and set him down next to his mother, then moved the woman's limp hand onto her child's belly to comfort him. The baby's eyes filmed over; he grew silent and passed through the moment's small doorway with a contorted face as though he kept crying in the beyond. Margery dropped a penny in his mouth.

Margery met a handsome man and told him the story of her life up to that moment, as though it held unique, coherent importance. A linear narrative, tunnel vision caused by fear. She was short but looked in his eyes. He was stirred like a lake by a deep current. Although his friends had died, plague and war enlarged his desire to stay alive. When this man had sex, he rocked inside, tipping back and forth rather than sliding in and out. He placed enough money in her palm for a few days.

To further her abasement, Wenslawe set Margery to serve a pauper whose unredeemed suffering is barely clothed in a story. Margery lived for three months in semi-darkness in the woman's third-floor tenement cell without bed or furniture, and slept under a cloak. A single mosquito stood on the ceiling. That's Jesus, she thought. Both women were infested with lice. To Margery's dismay their menstrual cycles linked so she was united with generic suffering, nameless and buried many times over.

The woman didn't cover her head; her gray hair was matted. Smoke from the unvented fire inflamed their eyes. Bumps on Margery's ankles became infected and they itched with swoony exasperation.

A black goat lay panting on its side in a murky corner—he was a sort of hearth to the women. The goat was so crippled by malnutrition that he walked on his front elbows. Margery carried water and sticks on her neck, begged for the woman's food and wine, and longed for Jesus. Because Margery was poor, every act demanded greater effort and her energy counted for less. Her tongue pushed around dry fibers of meat from diseased cattle and when the wine went sour she drank it herself from a stone cup.

Margery bought the woman a fancy meal with a gold coin that Mary had earned from begging. The goat watched slyly and Margery's own mouth watered as she laid out the salmon and shrimp (expensive in Rome even then), white bread, noodle pudding, and white beans cooked with mutton and onion, as though she were serving Jesus.

As Jesus, her guest touched the salmon. Margery pressed her tongue against her upper teeth to suggest how tasty it was.

An angel—gold space and wings like wilted lettuce leaves—turned away from the threshold: the angel of scrupulous despair who won't accept a false word in describing itself.

28

In early January at market in the Campo dei Fiori, Margery saw Dame Margaret Florentyne riding in a tiny car drawn by a white mule. The cold air held a yellow pall of ash. Margery stood in white rags, one hand resting respectfully on the mule's neck. Neither woman understood the other very well. Margaret noted everything attractive which affected the pace of her perception. She heard a wren's vehement warble. The mule nodded its big mallet head emphatically. Margaret's voice was artificially cheerful. *"Marjerya in poverté?"*

Margery considered the question, the brutal day-to-day grinding to dust. *"Grand poverté, madame."*

Margaret gathered the reins. *"Marjerya Sunday yes?"*

You can't have chance encounters unless you travel. Every table had a head waiter and two servitors but Margery sat at the high table where Margaret served her with her own hands.

Margaret wore golden hairpins, a silver belt, a slashed tunic, and a long red train. She had a parrot: green body, pink wingtips, and blue forehead; he bit his perch.

Margaret admired Margery's capacity. Feeling full made Margaret anxious as though something noisy had occurred.

She gave Margery a hamper with ingredients for a beef stew, filled her bottle with wine, and added eight balendine coins as well. Margery wept so hard she choked for air; her jaw distended and her eyes bulged. The parrot shrieked and splattered water in its bath and for some reason Dame Margaret clapped her hands.

It became fashionable to entertain Margery. Another Roman, Marcelle, asked her to dinner two days a week. He made a good living: they ate roasted quail stuffed with pomegranate seeds and marinated in honey; fritters of pike and eel mixed with dates, ginger, apricots, pine nuts, and parsley; an infusion of laurel and fennel; artichokes flattened out and fried; a comfit of squash, sugar, ginger, lemon, and honey; and fried custard, crisp and melting. *Hys wyfe was gret wyth childe*; pregnancy transformed her into a blood-lined nest. She wanted Margery to be godmother.

A single lady fed her on Wednesday, a blonde with big teeth and gold lashes who had a joyous love of company. For instance, in order to come she concentrated on fantasies in which three or four people attained together the utmost moment of pleasure.

The other days Margery begged from door to door. She was always hungry; as she lost weight her legs felt longer. She imitated Jesus's cold mobility when she walked. He was an incomprehensible silence.

29

As Margery, I wake up and enter the dark street hoping to catch a glimpse of Jesus and trying to avoid him. I miss him frantically but can't face his lack of interest. I didn't know I had a cunt till he wriggled his fingers inside me.

I'm ashamed of myself. Jesus must be seeing someone else: the speculation takes shape in the dark and I follow my replacement, losing and sighting him in narrow murky alleys. He has a huge craggy head, bald and ugly as Punch. Torches and candles cast halos in the acrid mist and beige moths circle the flames. The streets are noise but the moths are silence.

I tail my replacement to an alley that climbs to a stairway. He's shirtless; his massive torso is covered by square green scales like crocodile hide and he smokes a huge cigar whose weight makes him walk faster. Shadowy figures fold into each other and roil obscenely. I wonder if I've stumbled into a neighborhood orgy, body grinding against body. I want to wash my face and piss to simplify my congested feelings. I realize I'm wearing a veil—it's a dark threshold I step across into a town meeting. Citizens perch in tiers, the steps are bleachers. A woman complains, "When my boyfriend and I try to talk—"

I cut her off; I become the entire map of a problem from the slightest hint. I fall easily into the mode of telling them what to think and stand with my hands raised as though conducting an orchestra. Romantic dissatisfaction is the music. I remind the woman that talking reenacts

gender and class codes. Her boyfriend wants a shared ver-
bal rhythm, indifferent to content, while for her it's shared
observations that cement a bond. I had a similar problem
at dinner last night when—

An old man flings his arm into space and cries,
"Give up the dream of romantic ecstasy but believe it be-
longs to others with more luck. Twist your longing into
nostalgia for what's under your nose: a glass on the sill, geraniums in a pot." He's so old his head is horizontal. His
hair and beard are too long and he wears his gown unbelt-
ed with the huge buttons popular thirty years before. "Be old
and yearn for the visible which will not love you back. A day
at a time, an hour at a time. Can you *afford* physical joy?"

My open palms retain their hope but nothing
comes out of my mouth. His leathery face is hostile,
closed. A woman in front wears a headdress that spreads
above her ears; she turns in her seat and says to the group
in a taut voice, "My husband is only sorry when I'm crying.
'Well,' he says, 'you *stay* in the relationship.'"

Jesus's new lover brushes against me as he climbs.
Now he's as young as Jesus, with soft brown curls and Jewish features as aquiline as an arrowhead. He's serious, rich,
more troubled by my pain than Jesus is. He arouses me; I
can't breathe thinking of them together—the intaken
breath as a palm sweeps from armpit to thigh. Once sex is
entered they will divide between them the entire universe.

The old man climbs to his feet; every movement
must be planned in advance. He whinnies, *"How can I forgive the world till it says it's sorry?"*

My chest aches—a vehement tremolo—Jesus's new
lover melts in the shifting darkness. The Romans are

jumping up and talking all at once. My mouth hangs open; I gaze at the sky, deep night above the noisy court. A man points at me. "I'm *fucking* and I'm *drunk*. Continuous pleasure *meant* something,"—he pumps his fist as though jacking-off—"no future—the meaning's *gone.*"

I want to slow down these grievances but the Romans are incensed. Before I can look on the brighter side, the woman throws her hands up. "Do we *need* another story about *I'm in love with a god?*"

30

L. writes:

I guess I feel put on the defensive when I hear you talk about how you want me to be close to you because, while I understand your needs and desires, I don't think they take mine into account. On the surface it may look as though my life is much more flexible, yet for more than a year I've been trying to cement new beginnings that are important to me. If you really feel you won't be able to allow this to happen or wait before being together in a more continuous sense then we should really talk about it. I also hope you aren't assigning more importance to my sex thang the other night than it deserves. It was fun, no mess, and it made me feel closer to you. I'm happy for the time being. Attribute this to the end of winter, small gestures towards involvement, or the affirmation I have felt through you.

I asked my friends for notes about their bodies to dress these fifteenth-century paper dolls. I clothe the maid, Willyam Wever, the Archbishop of Lincoln in Camille's eruption of physicality, Ed's weekend of tears, Dodie's tangled nerve endings, Steve's afternoon nap. My story proceeds by interaction. My friends become the author of my misfortune and the ground of authority in this book. We are a village common producing images.

I borrow a story from Margery: I live on the Isle of Longo. The law of this land is the Longing for L. He enlarges me by not returning my love—wide deserts across which my being hurtles. I am the daughter of Hippocrates in the form of a dragon seven hundred feet in length, pure disguise in order to make a display. I turn my head and my weight beneath me coils the other way. And I shall endure in the form of a dragon until a knight come who is so hardy that he dare kiss me on the mouth.

L. has the short waist and long legs of a long-distance runner from the British Isles. His immaculate gym body is like a house so clean that no one has a real life there. I draw back to look at his asshole, bubble-gum-pink; there's a bead of balled-up paper lodged in a brown curl. I flick it away like a jaunty waiter brushing a crumb from the banquet table. He's sunk in a depression that paralyzes and terrifies him. For the last three months all he's done is look to other people for help. He's surprised by the pitch of my love. His features are sympathetic because frail. These descriptions support him as they consume him.

I follow him. He steals the value of my longing and rejects my fury and drab complaints. As he turns away I feel metal chains pull the gears of a clock in my chest. I raise my hands in a gesture of protection as my face subsides, the face of my elderly father.

31

When the Brothers of St. Thomas—who had kicked Margery out—heard of her success in Rome, they issued a new invitation. Margery returned to her room. Now the grapevines were bare and a rangy lizard clung to the brick wall.

Margery's maid also lived at St. Thomas; she lived well because she was the wine keeper. She performed her duties with watchful eyes and wore her good-looking body like clothes—a blue gown, tight above the waist and flowing below, with an oval neck and long tight sleeves. Margery begged from her and the maid was glad to help with food and wine; sometimes she dropped a groat in Margery's hand. The maid had shed her virginity: she was preoccupied by the moment when a monk's soft spike drove into her guts, so close their pubic hairs tangled.

They'd met in a tavern. Her clit had been too sensitive to touch. His cock poked her leg like a dog's nose. Wind whistled high in his throat. He spasmed shyly, laughing in embarrassment. For her, the event summoned an incomplete world. She didn't come but later, alone, added her own orgasms to a continuous replay of seizing his cock with her cunt. She did not want to marry; she shared Mrs. Noah's reluctance to board the ark. She probed her own truth, which hid in convulsions between her legs, wafting its aroma upwards. The monk had broken cloister; he'd found in her body and especially in her cunt an elegance he experienced as meaning.

On February 1, St. Bridget's Day, Margery tried to convince the maid to serve again. Unseasonal sunstorms bleached the sky to an eerie pallor. The maid mistook an ant crawling on her inner arm for a trickle of sweat; it moved on its own, a bead of exasperation. Her period was on its way so every insult and criticism was said for her benefit.

Heat emptied the streets. The plants' obvious joy in the toxic light exposed their alien and vaguely hostile nature. Clothes hung to dry were stiff in minutes. Jesus sent fluctuations that drove farmers in the fields to seek shelter. A blue mist smelling of sulfur rolled in and clouds gathered in the north. Thunder-startled pheasant cocks rocketed upwards in a whir, crowing a harsh *kor-kok*. Vast drops of rain were succeeded by round hail, then by pieces of ice three inches across; froth and spray stood four feet above the Tiber.

The storm continued all night; it dwindled to a drizzle, then exploded frantically. Hollow lanes were torn up; young trees whipped, old ones swayed slowly, and howling dogs traded their amazement. Jesus had warned Margery the night before not to go far from her lodging. Old men said they had never heard such thunder—the lightning radical and bright. Rome stood shadowless and cast out of the dark. By morning the air was mild, a tepid bath in which body shape was lost. A flash of blood on the toilet paper: the maid's period had begun. Pairs of gray ducks appeared in the flooded meadows, their quacks low and reedy.

A priest from England arrived bringing money for Margery. She was so relieved she told him the story of her life up to that minute. Her nipples and cunt were raw and alert from tasting Jesus, stretched and prickly, sweet and bosky. She ate with this priest and his party every day.

To discredit Margery, the pilgrims told the priest that a German who didn't know English had confessed her. Margery replied, *"Preyth hym to dyne wyth thow & wyth yowr felawys, & than xal thee knowyn the trewth."*

At dinner Wenslawe joined in when they spoke Latin. When they spoke English he sat with his big hands folded. He was overly sensitive of his body, its inexpressiveness. He wore a hood with a liripipe and chewed on the left side. They ate duck stuffed with ground duck, parmesan, pine nuts, and raisins. In August, eight months earlier, he'd cracked a molar biting on a stone in a dish of lentils while dining with his mother for the last time before she died. The darkness of centuries surrounded his bright shocks of pain. The devil invented teeth, he thought grimly.

Margery related the story of Elisha and the she-bear. When questioned, Wenslawe repeated the story in Latin because he understood English only from Margery. She could speak with anyone. So thank you, Jesus, you made a foreigner understand her when her own country-men abandoned her because she never stopped weeping and talking about you.

On Easter, 1415, the priest from England gave her enough money to return to Lynn. Margery said good-bye to Wenslawe and to her maid. The maid's moment of intensity was over; she stepped back to look like and die with her ancestors.

Margery sailed to Zealand. In Zealand they had a good wind to cross the channel, but they couldn't find a ship—only a little smack that had a well for live fish. The sailor at the helm became notes as he sang them. Margery wished she could sing as well; she was a little drunk on motion and spray. The wet brunt of the wind erased her problems. Drops struck her skin like beads of light. They lost sight of shore, the sky was gray, black; green waves pitched the tiny boat.

PART THREE
Her Being Was Hurtling

Sende down sum reyn er sum wedyr that may
throw thi mercy qwenchyn this fyre and esyn myn hert.

32

Margery landed in Yarmouth without a single penny. She did not want to be recognized because she was wearing a filthy canvas sheet. She held a handkerchief in front of her face until she could arrange a loan and buy some clothes. Then she walked quickly on the road to Norwich as though trying to keep up with Jesus. It was April; a woodpecker's drumming and its yelping cry. Pilgrims gave her a few coins for these stories:

A man drowns his pregnant wife in a pond, drags her out, and then has the cruelty to watch the motion of the infant still warm in her womb. The devil puts him up to it, appearing in a flash of lightning, and showing him where to find a hay spade to bury her with in a shallow grave by the pond. Easter Tuesday following, a man watering

97

a quickset hedge not far from his home, as he is going for a second pailful, an apparition before him sits on the grave: she seems to dandle something in her lap that looks like a white bag; she is pale, with her teeth visible but no gums. The man runs away so fast he yanks at the air.

Two ladies of quality love each other entirely. One of them falls sick with plague and desires to see the other, who will not come, fearing catching it. The afflicted at last dies, and has not been buried very long when she appears at the other's house dressed in mourning (for her own life). She asks for her friend, who is at cards, but sends down her maid to know her business, who tells her, *I must impart it to none but your lady,* who, receiving this answer, bids her maid to show her guest into a room, and asks her to wait till the game is done. Downstairs the lady comes to the apparition to know her business. *Madame,* says the ghost, turning up her veil (her face appearing full of craters), *you know very well, you and I loved entirely, and your not coming to see me, I took it so hard, at your hands, that I could never rest, till I had seen you, and now I am come, to tell you, that you have not long, to live, therefore, prepare to die, and when you are at a feast, and make the thirteenth person, in number, remember my words.*

33

Margery sent for John to meet her in Norwich. While waiting for him, she visited the Vicar of St. Stephen's. He had two years left to live as she had foretold nine years earlier. Still, Margery was shocked to find him wasting, his face small and dark, bony as a monkey's. He couldn't get warm; blue lids hooded his eyes. He thought, Wisdom is just subtraction. Her mirth filled him with longing for a world he was shrinking away from, and he could not reconcile her stamina with the sanctity of his death, his weighty marble sarcophagus.

He haunted his memories and hopes, rushing through them in a whisper. But sometimes his body gave him a moment of peace that could also be described as a whiff of sweet decay, like a dead mouse found in a trap. Then the world was artificial and his physical being seemed a less precious part of a richer and more compelling adventure. Sometimes he saw the spirit of a little boy jumping up and down on the bed. No sound, but shadows.

Margery said, "Jesus told me to buy a white mantle and robe."

The Vicar breathed, "Told you...?" The conversation ended as he climbed onto wobbly legs.

So Margery said, "Jesus, send me a sign for white clothes." She could not recognize herself apart from simple cues, the golden headdress of her youth or the mantle of lightning, thunder, and rain.

Early in the morning as she lay in bed, she saw the lightning, heard the thunder. A larch was instantly reduced to ashes. The first drops fell in pellets that sat on top of the hard dirt. Veins of lightning tangled in the distance. Mules sank in mud up to their pasterns; they brayed and lurched with their haunches. The tepid air went through an electrical cleansing. After the storm the decisive light laid a hand on her. No actual light could deliver such promise.

"But Jesus, I have no money to buy clothes."

He replied, "I'll buy them for you." Jesus always got money from someone else. He does own everything, she reasoned, but she had given her life and spent her fortune following him around, while nothing he gave made a difference in his life. In response, she grew more animated; that repelled Jesus, who took it as a demand. His somber character really didn't suit her; he barked orders and walked ahead. How long could she put up with that?

John set out from Lynn to take Margery home. He knew something was wrong—he pictured Jesus too clearly, saw Margery tipping onto him, two bodies then, and Jesus feels her weight which is given lightness by her breathing; she slides down a little, the tender flesh of her ass, two handfuls, the twin dimples at the base of her spine where muscles play; she nudges apart his long legs with small motions of her legs.

John thought, The world is getting smaller but not less frightening. Sheep, flies, and mosquitoes. He thought, Jesus is the devil. A scarecrow like an archer drew his bow. The smell of sun-baked dung. The chirping of the field insects ended as he entered the woods. Bright preindustrial blue through the trees. Families and journeymen, tramping or riding, carried their pieces of cloth to market. A goose raised its head for grain as a farmer swung his scythe—in the dust its yellow beak parted hopefully. Hawthorn bushes flowered and the sun arched over the open heaths. A blackbird with a yellow bill ran in a crouch.

Margery met John on the street outside her inn—a spring dusk of lilting clarity. He had not seen her in over a year: he swung around her like a dancing bear and beamed love that was consoling and hard to endure. She was very glad to see him. John didn't care about judgments or personalities, his own or others'.

John believed in sensation and agreement. Agreement led him to farmers markets and dog races, to parties where everyone said hello and started jumping halfway to the dance floor. Sensation led him to alcohol and bodies. He thought if drink didn't bloat him it would have been a wonderful invention—perhaps the only one—of Mother Nature. He slept with women who looked like Margery, ruddy and small: that was the form his vow of chastity had taken. He couldn't come till he cried *I love you* in his mind. He'd lie still, blackness passing upwards, feet jiggling as though he were being hanged.

They ate in a tavern fumy with dry sherry and wine. Margery stuck out in her white mantle. She described marrying Jesus in a voice that was too bright. John sagged against her; he looked sick; he finally understood they would not be together. His face broke open. His wide mouth gaped, the muscles stood rigid on his neck, and his big forehead sank onto her shoulder—the huge doleful head of a steer. He cried strongly, imagining himself curled in a ball. Sobs jerked his body. Margery stroked his thick hair; she was also sad.

Margery considered the mahogany hair that swept down his forearms. She was forty-one and John was over fifty. "John, why do you love me?" It was a thoughtless question, cruel.

John's hand brushed hers; warmth rippled from forefinger to elbow. She had been unhappy so long she wondered what part of themselves happy lovers give up. John replied hopefully, "You are beautiful, and your little teeth, and intelligent, your nipples, and you have a great sense of—" Margery cut him off. She knew the list. It didn't touch her terror or the Margery who needed proof that she would not be abandoned.

In Lynn she noted who was still alive; she fell ill and lay immobile, profoundly inside her body, painfully apart from it. Her skin prickled down her front from scalp to toes: it was a form of anticipation. Each minute she thought, This might be it.

34

Instead of moving upwards as it recedes, the ground rushes straight into me. Now there's a racket like an uproar of birds from some mechanism in the rear. Then a second high whine. I haven't developed an aesthetic of patience the way others do as they age. Lights come on, all dark outside, our heads erect against our upright seats. The blue lights of the landing strip and the distant, radiant terminal.

The forward momentum of my longing becomes a form of velocity, membranes and aspirations surging towards a foreign airport, its degraded earth empty of meaning except direction towards a hotel room where I erotically dismantle him. Heaven is the total presence at once of my self and my body. It's my own skin I travel towards—its *entire arousal* a homecoming, effortless freedom.

Almost two years had passed since Margery returned from Rome. She was poor and in debt. Three feet of snow covered Lynn; Margery was so cold she became bewildered; she heard the trilling *shree* of a waxwing. The wind deprived her of breath and swatted tears off her face. Some said she had epilepsy because she turned blue as lead. They spat at her in horror of disease. Some said she howled like a dog.

Margery wanted to see the shrine of St. James at Santiago Compostela. She told her friends, "Jesus will give me money," but he delayed until midsummer.

Lynn's gardens abounded with solstitial flowers: roses, cornflags, orange lilies, pinks, and yellow honeysuckles so fragrant they perfumed the street. Willow down filled the air. A linnet warbled in a tuft of hazel trees. The yellow wheat, the fresh grass. A couple sheared sheep; brown wool accumulated at their feet. The horizon lacked incident, an irrigation ditch, a wash of clouds only slightly whiter than the sky.

She arrived in Bristol on May 26, 1417, and waited six weeks. Henry V had requisitioned all ships for his second expedition. The beach seemed pressured, empty; the small waves exasperated Margery with their demand for attention that, once given, offered nothing to attend. Fishermen laid out nets to dry in the wind. Mobility and chance were beginning. Sanderlings pattered along the foamy edge. Moving randomly through the world canceled the agreement between space, time, and Margery's body. Jesus taught her to make angels; they lay on their backs and dragged their arms in the sand to shape wings. Then they turned over, serious and happy, groins and faces pressed into the warmth.

The city was full of soldiers; there was a campaign to suppress heretics before the attack on France. Margery said a prayer before bed to give her unconscious a list of problems to work on.

A ship was ready to sail to Compostela—a little galley high of prow and stern. The sailors believed Margery controlled the weather so one of them warned her they intended to throw her overboard if a storm hit. Dark clouds covered the sky; the water was lumpy as flint. Pale fulmars followed the ship in stiff flight for seven days.

Margery and Jesus stayed two weeks in Compostela. Rain fell steadily on the city's head; water spilled down stone gutters and into the granite streets. Glittering drops in Jesus's hair and lashes. Margery was never dry. They watched a white goose in a maze, its head bobbing just above the box hedge. It waddled forlornly in the rain, turning corners, backtracking, until it sauntered out of the puzzle.

No matter how fast Margery trotted on her short legs to catch up, Jesus strode a yard ahead with the pre-occupied frown of someone late, face tossed back as though from the speed. He denied Margery the companionship he was providing. Later he let her drink rain off his skin. When the sun appeared for an hour of immensity, canaries trilled vehemently in their little cages on the windowsills.

L. and I face a large lawn. He protests, "I show affection in different ways—" I consider the possibilities: his hand on my shoulder guided me around a corner, his knee fell against mine—were they more than I thought? Our union makes more sense to L. outside New York and San Francisco, an isolation in which he feels tenderness and separation at the same time.

The lawn has a head of grass that has attained Flamboyant Gothic consciousness, bunched up against the foundation of an arbor. The gardener, unaware, smooths out the alarmed head and flattens it beneath the arbor. The grass thinks, This is fine, calming itself, but realizes that no sun can reach it: *I will slowly die.*

While I daydream, L. talks about his art, a friend's memorial—nothing I can focus on. His actual life moves too slowly.

We eat yellow pepper soup, mushroom salad, and chocolate pine-nut cake. People in the restaurant look at him. Later he strips and blindfolds me. He runs a fingertip across my cock creating and denying expectation till I float in a cosmos of emptiness and touch. When I leave our bed

I crouch a little, hoping the dimples on my ass will disappear. The extremes are captivating: exalting pleasure and the harshest judgment in that my own contempt works in his name. My legs are shaky. I step into the big room. The air is oddly empty. By contrast, I'm aware of my flesh and the thick stew it's been for an hour or more.

35

Margery landed in Bristol on July 9. The weather was good, and travel itself was an authentic place to speak from—where events unfold, the crest of duration. She stopped in Leicester on her way home and found a room at an inn.

As Margery entered the church, Jesus pushed past her through the door; he knocked her off balance and gloated over his shoulder as though he'd won a contest. She had not seen him since Compostela. They sat down. Her desire to be young conflated with his cruel immaturity, as though rough manners were a promise of youth. Margery was forty-three. But Jesus didn't lead a youth gang; he was thirty-one, so he was lying too. She held the corner of her cloak elegantly to alert Jesus to each finger's tapering. He could have told her the gesture was out-of-date.

Four girls squatted in the corner projecting their world onto little half-naked bodies which they twisted intently; then one of the girls held her doll up, suddenly animate, so it could speak to the others.

What is there to these dolls besides moments of arousal followed by emptiness? Jesus announced in a stern parental voice, "There is much sorrow coming to you."

Margery was silent. Is pain more convincing than pleasure? The best prophet is the assassin. She couldn't see into the assassin's face—eyes blank, mouth drawn downwards.

Margery experienced the camaraderie of the dolls as remorse without an object. Jesus shrugged, "If you don't want my love..." She was bewildered. With John, Margery had duplicated her parents' marriage, so Margery was strong; Jesus shrank her down to a child, adoring and lost, perhaps unloved. He called for unconditional surrender—but to what? Raising his palm in an oddly formal salute, he disappeared.

Margery would have been surprised to learn how badly assembled Jesus was. Lacking all external criticism, he was vague even to himself. His visits should have replaced the stream of life with something conclusive—or was his incoherence the attraction? She foresaw the catastrophe though no words passed. In fantasies Jesus showed need and intent in his touch but his actual hands lay lifeless and she tried to prop them up over her back. She made it into a game, "Jesus the Puppet." If he didn't respond to her body, he might respond to her joke?

Even when Margery bathed him, he wouldn't let her caress his nipples or his gleaming belly. It's painful to describe. She used shrewdness to hide her humiliation from both of them. His coldness was a greater problem than any believable solution; she preferred fraud and Jesus, yet she complained constantly.

No, but *I* was torn up with loneliness—I say as my puppet says it too. A still beam of sunlight pierces a dark tumultuous fountain, a kind of exultation I can only grasp through the pleasure it might give L. I can't know it except through him. I have no position—what can *I* reject? My body seems large, my skin blushes and reaches in every direction for contact with L.'s skin. I raise my eyes to a dark window seven stories high where L. lives in New York. The window is lit, he is flesh and blood, he leans into another man in amusement and then warmth. I whisper his name to elevate this story with the strength of my sexuality.

36

In Leicester on a porch invaded by honeysuckle the ostler's in-a-blue-shift daughter made a circle with her hands and brought them over her head without unclasping. Margery knew that the girl had recently acquired an acute sense of smell and was almost always aware of the scent of her own cunt. Open, blood, fold. When the girl saw her sister's clitoris she said, "Mine's bigger than hers."

Eggs began drifting through fallopian wastelands. The girl liked to stroke her newly growing breasts but when she lay on her stomach they hurt. She was always tempted to run away; she got to the front gate and looked up through wild eyes at Margery, who told her she would have a lot of pleasure in life if she lasted that long.

The girl's father, the ostler, ran up to Margery's room and grabbed her bag. The Law was etched into his very grain. He wouldn't let Margery finish a letter (she was asking John to take her home because traveling alone was dangerous). She had a dubious reputation. Like any fanatic, she needed to show the world what she had become. She could have avoided trouble; instead she harangued people, an unlicensed preacher, maybe subversive.

The ostler was a thin-limbed man with a potbelly and a pointed nose; he was never far from sleep. He rushed Margery to the Mayor through narrow streets that led to the guildhall. The ostler was worried about the future. It was his duty as a citizen to protect the state against heretics now that the King was away unleashing English power.

They came to an iron pole he'd used to climb; he'd gone up and slid down, gone up again and again until a kind of orgasm rushed between his thighs. He pressed his face against the metal, a steely scent, musty and gray. Death was learning to speak. Cobblers, harnessmakers, potters, glovers, gilders, spicers, smiths, and skinners— they worked harder and harder but their labor was a kind of apathy (their isolation and equivalence were the ostler's dreams materialized).

Peasants danced in a churchyard to a hurdy-gurdy, arms and legs thrown out like swastikas. Margery could not believe her eyes; her indignation kept them dancing night and day for a whole year. Her miracle was mean spirited. They danced themselves waist deep into the ground.

The Mayor was an ash blond with perfectly chiseled features. The words *hello* or *please* cost him too much to be wasted on Margery: as soon as he saw her he cried, *"Dic mihi nomen amantis."* The devil could answer difficult questions in good Latin. "How should *crescite et multipli-camini* be understood?" Heretics said it justified free love. Priests stood around to hear her reply and a soldier leaned on a pike with a sprocket.

"Speak English. I don't understand what you are saying."

"Speak *English*. Speak *English*." He minced as though lying were lecherous. "You are a *liar* in plain English."

He would have been stunning but his nervous mouth always chewed on his cheek. *"I will burn you—whore, Lollard, deceiver of the people!"* He expected Margery to fall on her face and beg.

She said, *"I am as redy, ser, to gon to preson as thee arn redy to gon to chirche."*

"Ah," said the Mayor with a meaningless smile.

Margery climbed to a privy in the prison tower. In company she was bright with expression but alone, smiling still, her teeth started chattering; the vibration reminded her of her skull.

There was a window she could put her face through. She saw orchards crowded beneath blond hills, city walls, and people laughing and pointing at her, saying, "Amazing, amazing." The window's position was a town joke and Margery became part of the joke's folklore: the holy woman with her ass on the pot and her face in the clouds. Margery hoped Jesus wouldn't hear of that, but she also laughed.

The Mayor took Margery by the hand and led her into his chamber; he told her he wanted to lick her breasts, that his cock was stiff and he wanted her to taste it.

"Sir, I am the daughter of a man who was mayor five times." He rubbed himself and wet his lips. Margery felt giddy, that her body betrayed her by blushing.

"Tell me whether you talk with Jesus or the devil." His breath was labored.

The Mayor repeated the question to himself that night when continuous rain pounded Leicester. People said it rained because he had thrown Margery in prison.

37

On the second Wednesday of July, Margery was brought to the Church of All Hallows before the high altar where the Abbot of Leicester and some canons were seated. There were friars, priests, and townsfolk who came to see if Margery would be burnt—so many they jostled and scrambled onto stools. They were coarse: a wave of acrid sweat, faces and hands added later.

The Mayor cried, "Silence!" and the Abbot put his spectacles on and looked around to see who was talking. The Mayor wore a blue silk mantle with an orange border. He wondered if the fear in Margery's eyes when she saw him was mirrored in his own.

Margery knelt before the altar and raised her palms in the position of piety. It was a scene from a penny broadside, the clumsy perspective jumble, the figures partaking of the wooden block that made them.

The Mayor asked, "What have you done with the baby conceived in adultery and spawned when you were abroad?"

Margery was thunderstruck. Slander had thrown its spear decked with ears. The charge of sedition often is framed as a sexual crime. "Sir," she said, "I never had part of any man's body in *this* world excepting John Kempe's by whom I have borne fourteen children."

"She does not mean with her heart what she says with her mouth!" The Mayor was so full of grievance he stepped from side to side like a boxer. The Lollards were gaining strength in his city. He was rich and uncomprehending, surprised that anyone would object to being mistreated by him. "Why do you dress in white? You have come to lure our wives from us and lead them off."

Margery snorted. He was accusing her of being one of the Flagellant Albi who roamed from town to town whipping themselves. "You are not worthy to know why I wear white but if the court were cleared of laymen, I would tell the clerics as though in confession."

Than the clerkys preyd the Meyr to gon down fro hem wyth the other pepyl. The Mayor's voice grated with rage. "I will not let you go in spite of anything until you get a letter from my Lord Bishop of Lincoln—you are in his jurisdiction."

Margery shouted, "I am no heretic." She hid her hands under her mantle; she did not know how compelling she was—her certainty aroused Jesus.

The Abbot of Leicester looked more like God than

Jesus's father, with fierce circumflex eyebrows and fiery red eyes. He glared at Margery and asked with rich indignation, "Are you a Christian or a Jew, a woman or not?" Margery tilted her head as Jesus sang:

> *The kiss you gave me,*
> *Burning and bold,*
> *Ran off with two birds,*
> *And flew to their tree,*
> *To guard their nest*
> *From the cold.*

Her delight was startling because so inappropriate. She tipped her ear to contain his voice and felt the warm sensation of hearing that comes before orgasm.

> *What can I do but whisper this,*
> *And beg you for another kiss?*

She dropped to the floor, face churning, tears falling. A black-hooded church doctor declared, "It's all her fancy; she has no sorrow."

The Abbot snarled, "Be quiet!" The doctor shriveled as though to escape a blow. The Abbot asked Margery, "Why do you weep?" His face was lightning looking for ground.

"You will wish...some day...you wept...as sorely as I."

"I hear you are a wicked woman."

"I hear you are a wicked man. If you are as wicked as they say, you'll never get to heaven."

"Why you...what do people say?"

"Other people, Sir, can tell you." She flushed with power on the infinite point she was making.

"She speaks against the Church," the doctor complained. "She told me the worst story I ever heard."

Margery climbed to her feet, expanding on the limitless plane of her voice. "A priest got lost in a forest. He found an arbor with a young pear in the middle covered in blossom. A huge bear, ugly and rank, shook the tree till the blossoms fell. The bear ate all the flowers, turned his tail, and sprayed the priest with watery shit.

"The priest was disgusted and very depressed because he could see the shit was symbolic. He met a handsome old man who asked the priest why he was sad. The priest repeated the matter: rank beast devours blossoms and sprays them horribly out its ass.

"The old man explained: You act without faith. You sit over your beer, give yourself up to your body…"

"I don't believe there's a crumb of sense in it," the doctor stated.

The Abbot thought, I would give twenty pounds to have her tears. He said hopelessly, "That's a good story."

Quick stages of demolition and reconstruction replaced one another on the doctor's face. He said, "Good story," submissive.

Margery nodded with pleasure. "If anyone dislikes it, watch him—he's guilty."

"Who will escort this woman to the Bishop of Lincoln?" A young man jumped up; he had a deer's passionate eyes, edible flesh, and furry rump. He was still preoccupied by the growth of his cock during puberty. The Abbot said, "Too young."

Thomas, a somber man of the court, asked, "What will you give me?" His eyes were set so close in his narrow face they made you dizzy. The Abbot offered five shillings and Thomas demanded a noble.

"Here are five shillings. Escort her quickly out of this area."

38

Philip, Bishop of Lincoln, had presided over Margery's vow of chastity. First she went to Leicester Abbey and into the church. A peacock angel opened a manderla in the bulging air in which Jesus sat naked on his three-legged stool. She was used to swallowing him whole. Anticipation elongated her body and arched her forehead. Jesus walked towards her; his milky skin was so fine his veins were visible. Her knees buckled, she held onto a pillar and felt as though she were running. The unruly outside was sucked into her body with her breath. He was grinding every grain of separate existence to dust. A thick swarm buzzed louder towards a longed-for and intolerable crescendo; the excitement was also a light sense of well-being that tapered her fingers and lifted her lips and nipples. She was moved but also disturbed by his torso, a face without features. Jesus lowered his lids and tipped his head back, basking and effeminate. Two tiny points of hair on his chin were his beard. She questioned her attraction and answered yes, it was strong.

The next day Thomas brought her to the Bishop's palace. Philip was still in bed. In his hall men stood in clothes fashionably slashed and cut into points. They were dandies; they wore jeweled circlets on their heads and fluffed their hair out around their ears; their gowns ended above the crotch and they wore particolored hose with long pointed toes. Their gestures expressed cordiality, delight, disarming confusion, throwing caution to the wind. Margery's attention was specific and random as a flashlight beam loosely dragged across her century.

Finally the Bishop entered, wearing a jerkin of otter skin and a plain green cloak. He circulated among his guests, isolated in his mannerisms, existing entirely at the level of delighted greetings and a rush of compliments. He squirmed with pleasure to see Margery and asked after John. Her old affection for John surfaced as remorse—his tremulous sweetness and the purity of his open face.

Philip insisted that she was doing him a favor by accepting his letter. He invited her to dine with him.

It was disconcerting to be with someone so happy. Philip sat with his back to a huge fireplace; sparks flew upwards above a round plaited fire screen. Mint and fennel were strewn on the floor to sweeten the air. His pantler and carver stood by and his cup bearer poured French wines. His cup bearer was so young that when he came his body arched like the swag of fruit that dangled above Philip's head. Margery joyfully ate cherries, then white bread, fresh beans boiled in milk, roach and crab, eel pasties, rice cooked with milk of almonds and cinnamon, lampreys baked with a sauce, tarts, new cheese, and fruit.

Margery asked Philip, as though in confession, "Which way should I go from here?"

Philip shook his face as though clearing away cobwebs of sleep. Her question was entirely novel. He furrowed his brow and pressed one finger against his forehead in exaggerated thought while Margery waited in silence. Finally he said, "That depends on where you want to get to." The Bishop vanished quite slowly: the darkness of time was the darkness of unconscious life. Margery talked more urgently as his face faded and white stars began to shine through it. The air became white; the sky was yanked up at the corners. Heavy storms flattened the crops and blew petrels inland, where they fluttered on gray wings like bats above the ponds. His grin grew wider after the rest had gone, expression without context.

Horses waded belly deep into the water to crop the grass floating on the surface. In Leicester, thunder soured the beer. The Mayor grew lean with fright: the storm tore branches off old trees and the devil ripped the Mayor's soul out and flew away holding its corner at arm's length like a dirty napkin flapping in the wind.

When the Mayor read the Bishop's letter, he returned Margery's bag and instructed Thomas to take her home. People wanted her to leave that part of the country. She walked a few steps ahead as Jesus did, but no further because, unlike Jesus, she needed her audience in earshot. She would go to heaven on a path running through the minds of Thomas and others who listened. The Mayor had detained her for three weeks.

39

L., as Jesus, lounges on his side and unbuttons the fly of his gray rayon slacks; he fishes out his cock and balls and drapes them across his thigh to the mattress so their exposure isolates their pendulousness. His lip, snagged on a tooth, duplicates the shape of his cock's ragged mouth. A pale band of skin between his shirt and trousers was dented by the elastic of his boxer shorts. He's controlling his breath. Infinitely passive, he's subject himself to the clamor his body makes. He pushes my hand away.

Although I travel, I'm deflected from my goal. I never encountered nakedness that was not also an invitation. My heart beats with useless excitement. He struggles to understand a rage inside himself. Is my love amazing because it exists? Does it verify my existence or are my tears merely the faulty plumbing of an hysteric? L.'s cock testifies to the human form he chose—so strange to him that he will not let me touch it, as though keeping co-conspirators from meeting.

Thomas was unhappy like steady rain; he could barely keep up with Margery. He had a sore on his tongue, a hard kernel that was killing him. The August sky was clear with a white cloud range to the south. Margery needed to keep moving, to re-predicate herself in different contexts.

Two yeomen blocked her path. One leaned on the staff of his lance, the other draped his hand on the pommel of his sword. Margery said, "Whose men are you?"

They opened their palms in explanation, "The Duke of Bedford's men!"

The Duke of Bedford was Henry's brother and, in the King's absence, the most powerful man in England. Fourteen years later, in 1431, Joan of Arc would be burned under Bedford's eye for false enchantments and sorcery. His yeomen wore studded green-leather crossbelts and their teeth were blue from eating blackberries.

One smelled his blue finger and put it in his mouth. He had a pressing memory: after they'd had a swim, his partner pushed his legs over his head and rimmed him. He had writhed, amazed by a cool shifting fire closer to wherever it was that he was than any other sensation. He thought his friend had broken the rule against worshiping idols. They'd been so rattled they gazed into each other's eyes with unguarded expressions.

The yeomen led Margery and Thomas northward towards Beverly, where the Duke of Bedford was holding court. *"For owr Lord hath sent for thee, & you art holdyn the grettest loller in al this cuntre, & we xal han an hundryd pownde for to bryng thee be-forn owr Lord."* She went unwillingly; there was plague in Beverly—would she die for no reason? Yet this actual threat of death was separate from the fear that always gnawed at her.

Larks, throstles, blackbirds, linnets, and cuckoos poured out music on every side. When Thomas pissed, he lifted his cock from the top by the scruff of its foreskin like a pup. The road was roughly paved with large stones and it cut across green billowing wolds. Blue-toothed women with their distaffs ran out of their houses crying, "Burn this heretic!" Margery felt the cool spray of their words. They had no scale to measure difference: Margery's white mantle was a sexual crime, a revolution, a collapse of meaning.

Beavers still lived in the riverbanks, swatting the water with their tails. Two columns of smoke appeared static as though supporting the sky. People said, "Woman, give up this life, go and spin, card wool, and don't endure so much shame and bitterness."

Margery told stories to Thomas and to the yeomen who had arrested her: her faith in language exceeded theirs but the spectacle of that belief gave them the consolation of believing their own lives had value.

The yeomen were bald with pale blue eyes and red mustaches. One would die in 1421—a death in which one person dies for all—and the survivor would look at his friend's corpse before mass. The heat that *was* his friend was still retreating. The yeoman was a little frightened of dead people, but the face did not turn brown or blue and when the yeoman met his friend's cold hand for the last time there was no fear. He said, "We're just the same body—and should I be afraid of *myself?*"

Later, his tears appeared so simply they surprised him. His body didn't clench, there were no spasms. He just stepped outside and sat for a while so quietly that he could feel the tears well up and spill on their own as though they were part of the day along with the weedy yard and the yellow light falling on a retaining wall.

40

In Beverly, Margery's purse and the ring Jesus had given her were impounded. Thomas was thrown in prison but the jailer volunteered to keep Margery at his own house. They cut across a broad common where cows lay beneath the twin towers of the minster. She smelled clover and dried milk. The jailer kept jabbing her between the shoulder blades. He had a guilty relation to people. On his hearth sat a dish of white bread sopped up with milk to appease the fairies. He put her in a fine room and from her window she told stories so compelling that women wept and cried, "Why should you be burnt?"

Margery asked the jailer's wife for a drink. "My husband took the key." The jailer fantasized during sex—it made him feel guilty so he fantasized about his wife. She would try to be more present but it never worked, never ever, so what is there to the mind-body continuum?

The jailer's wife: a hot flash—sweat broke out across her brow. She set a ladder against the window and brought Margery a pot of wine and a cup and asked her to conceal them. Margery filled the cup so high she had to lean over to drink. She plucked hair from her chin, between her breasts, and on her upper thighs. Sometimes her physicality seemed like an eruption through the feminine rather than into it.

She sat by the window and imagined Jesus. He's talking about her to Mary, to a saint. He wants to please her. Children played tag into the dusk on a lawn, in an alley beside it, and up a wall they scaled with a ladder permanently left there for them. Their mild shouts echoed on the green. (When Margery was a girl she ran so fast her legs didn't support her and she collapsed. This memory seemed to occur outside the social order. She had felt extraordinary power in running, a feeling her body could not sustain.)

The air was soft and chickens settled in the boughs of the apple and quince. The scene was timeless because it had no shadows. The more chaotic Margery's life became, the more she longed for Jesus. Her anticipation amplified the world as it took a last look at its own blue sky with the greed of the visible. She raised her palm in his rather somber salute. A few stars appeared, serenely actual, and a few bats. Her longing was so direct it seemed kinetic, a power expanding on itself. She sat up in bed in the darkness. Her heart beat painfully. She was surprised to be alone. He owed her what she needed, the commitment of his nakedness for her to endlessly unveil.

A loud voice blew a chill into her bones: *Margery.* She awoke clammy and spooked and lay still. Jesus glided out of the dark with underwater fluency; he was resplendent in a short crimson gown, a large velvet hat trimmed with lynx, a golden girdle around his waist, and a golden baldric trailing behind. He wore a sassy expression, head tossed to one side, shoulders cocked. His sap green breeches were so tight she thought his asshole appeared when he bent over; she was more aware than Jesus of that blurred red light in the darkness. What began as a fashion show ended as a striptease.

When they were about to come, Margery spit in his open mouth.

"That's gross," Jesus whispered with a look of grievance.

"Of course it is," Margery replied in a normal voice as Jesus began to spasm with a weak unwilling groan, shifting beneath her slightly. Margery was giving Jesus something to remember but it was Margery who remembered it. "We had exchanged so much spit but let some fly through the air... It was just something I wanted to give him."

41

People do not like Margery during their lifetimes but want her to weep when they are dying and she does because she thinks of Jesus dying. Jesus shapes her dread and expresses the ecstasy of the present.

She pushes her finger into his asshole as though he's a pie. She encounters shit—well, it's Jesus's shit; she just slides it out of the way. She nudges his prostate while pressing down on his groin with her palm, mixing the inside and outside. This makes Jesus moan though Margery isn't sure if he's responding to the sensation or the idea. Only his asshole has odor—a dragon guarding the cave. Once inside, she's elsewhere—underwater though able to breathe. My cathedral is built for a god to see so even secret places have ornament.

His pubic hair looks adolescent; his cock looks big, big, big—big head, big shaft, lots of skin, and looks like it could get bigger.

It's my cock Bob is describing. Bob licks his lips to articulate its pleasure. I put a "do not" sign on the door... turn the lock... tip him over. His body an Eden... his mind inhabits... illegally... till I enter. I fill his ass... yet stay soft... till the moment... I come... pliable... spongy... big enough... to strike... all his nerves... as though... a tongue pushed... in all directions... against... his inner walls... larger... than history ... now... he's completely... awake... yet free... of dread... groaning... continuous... release. Cramped in... that position ... his legs... go to sleep... to his waist. As they wake... I wonder... do his neighbors... think... his groans... are bliss? He laughs... in confusion... his ass... clenched... his head... wobbling... a top... slowing... the possibility... of falling... sperm on... the old carpet. I can't reconcile... the tenderness... of my flesh... with the coolness... of my manner. He's agitated... broken... attentive. I don't know... how to be... around this ... remain loving... while continuing... to assert... we are breaking... up. I ascend... foreshortened... the air... is hot... dust ... from the ceiling... makes me sneeze... my ears... itch. Bob is... still vibrating. To infer... long from short... is pleasant ... but he can't... do without... me on earth.

42

Next morning Margery was brought by the two yeoman to the chapter house in Beverly. The Archbishop of York was presiding because the Duke of Bedford, learning of a Scottish incursion, had collected an army and marched north. The Archbishop entered the hall with his clerics. He wore a small cap and a scarlet cape with slashes for his white-sleeved arms. A few weeks before, he had marched at the head of several thousand of his tenants against the Scots. A severe man, he could still hear drums roll across the moors.

Seeing Margery's wet emotional face, the Archbishop cried, "Why do you go around in white? Are you a virgin?"

Impatience was an ingredient in all his actions. He complained to the assembly, "I have a number of deaths to deal with. They had this woman before the Abbot of Leicester and found no fault in her. He gave one of his men five shillings to lead her out of this part of the country: they were arrested, the man thrown in prison, her gold and silver taken away, and here she is. Who says anything against her?"

A Franciscan with a huge nose stepped forward and took Margery's wrist. He had molten bars in his cheeks but his touch was so cold she jerked her arm back to her side. He claimed she disparaged all men of the Church, that a heretic with her name was burnt at Lynn, that she was a Lollard spy, that she had never been to Jerusalem.

The Archbishop rolled his eyes.

The friar licked his teeth. "My lord, she knows her faith. Still, my Lord of Bedford is angry with her."

"Well, friar, you can escort her to him."

Later she was led into the Archbishop's chamber. A green arras was worked with the image of three girls. His prostate ached after a strangely painful shit. Green fustian blankets covered his legs and his sheets were embroidered with dots and tendrils.

The friar came forward. His nose cast its shadow to one side. The friar saw himself as especially cooperative. He asked questions, but he was so eager to be right that he substituted the answer he wanted to hear. The Archbishop said, "Now say while she is present what you said when she was not present."

"Shall I?"

"Yes," said the Archbishop.

"You advised my Lady Greystoke to leave her husband, and she is a baron's wife, and daughter to my Lady of Westmorland."

They all turned to Margery. "I told her about a lady who gives her sweetheart a collection of miniature books—and they are delightful in his castle library. He decides to collect more and when she sees he has chosen larger volumes she runs crying from the room; her sleeves fly out and strike both sides of the doorway."

The Archbishop was laughing and angry. His steward and household threw out their hands. "Let her go—if she ever comes back we will burn her ourselves."

"No woman in England was ever so treated as she is." To Margery the Archbishop added, "I don't know what to do with you."

"Let me have your letter and seal, and let Thomas bring me to the river." The Archbishop returned her purse, amazed at the money it held. Actually, Margery had lost her fortune traveling with Jesus and needed supporters to give her money. Like most poor people, she carried all her savings with her.

Thomas and Margery passed a rickety nag pulling an empty wagon; its owner was a ghost who clung to a spoke to keep from spilling into nothingness. They heard bloodhounds and boarhounds barking and a hunter blowing the mort. A red-faced apothecary ate spiders as greedily as nuts because he was crop sick. The long grass was green except, oddly, along the bank of the Humber where it was brown.

Thomas left Margery there, taking the Archbishop's letter with him. The oarsman's shadow stood on the river's surface.

43

Margery returned to Lynn where a man threw a bowl of water on her head as she walked down the street.

She had dysentery; she couldn't hold a spoon; she wandered around her room on hands and knees, hiding from stabbing pain that wrung endless cries from her while searing diarrhea exploded down her thighs. It took all her concentration to breathe. White clumps of pus formed at the back of her throat; an appetite would have been ironic since she couldn't swallow her spit.

Memories of her excesses nauseated her as distant roads fell into each other again and again like taffy. At the limit of exhaustion the strong bright structures caved in. She'd always been strenuously on the move by ship, on foot, on horse. Now, alone in her room, her eyes raised indifferently. Yet lying in bed wasn't boring. Dying became an activity full of lively interest. Just *observing* her fragility admitted endless variations. As she gained strength she was reborn to appetite and movement.

Another illness followed; it settled in her right side below her ribs lasting all but eight weeks of eight years. Sometimes it struck Margery once a week lasting thirty hours, sometimes twenty, sometimes ten, sometimes eight, sometimes four, sometimes two, so hard and sharp that she threw up. John held her head; her lips drew back from the taste of bile.

Her priest gave her Jesus's body hidden in bread. Her head tipped back and emitted little groans from the bottom of the throat where her membranes were shores touched by a distant sea. Then Margery cried as if soul and body parted; she screamed as much as it hurt; two men held her arms. Jesus appeared above, a thin cloud behind his bony head looked like it traveled through his ears; his neck was as wide as his face and so beautifully modeled it was also expressive. She *saw* Jesus turn away; she *tasted* Jesus restore her from within. People outside heard her: *I die, I die.*

Jesus looked at her, experimenting with her absence: she pulled in her shoulders, suddenly chilled by the clay she was made of; she held her breath, aroused by her own inconsequence. He told her who would die. Margery covered her ears; she couldn't believe it was Jesus so he withdrew in exasperation, leaving inordinate lust in his place.

Rabbis, imams, and priests appeared in a grove of huge yews and showed her the tears of pre-come on their erections. Satan thundered (the shock waves hit her chest): YOU MUST CHOOSE WHICH ONE YOU WANT—NO—YOU MUST PROSTRATE YOURSELF BEFORE ALL. Satan had boar fangs and bark-colored skin; his balls were coconuts, hairy and brown, and his cock was knotted to keep it from dragging. Fragrant wild thyme covered the ground and random lights swept across their bodies. Her pubic mound itched—a maddening sharp jabbing. She liked one of the men better than the others. She could not say no; she had to do it; he plunged into her in a hollow tree, her nipples and face grinding against spongy wood, musty and sweet as testicle skin.

Satan ordered her to come; flames jumped up and down her groin and thighs and through her asshole; she wriggled and jerked against her will like a manic puppet, her muscles tugging the man's cock so hard it passed the point of no return. When his straining body also reached the breaking point, his helpless cries began and Satan made her moan, "It's heaven!"

She laughed with shame yet excitement made everything arousing seem normal. Out of sheer spite a demon did a backflip. Satan's voice almost ripped her ears off: AS HIS DAUGHTER YOU DISAPPOINT, AS HIS MOTHER YOU EXASPERATE, AS HIS SISTER YOU ARE BULLIED, AS HIS WIFE YOU ARE ABANDONED—so deafening it killed the world.

A cuckoo echoed far off, then near. Satan's furnace-mouth gaped wide and the terror of being swallowed drew her on a conveyer towards his jaws as her feet whirred in front like a clown on ice.

"Jesus, you said you would never abandon me!" Margery felt like a balloon full of water, easily punctured, webbed with a tangle of charged nerve endings, prickly in the slightest breeze—an unbelievable pressure inside that wanted to slosh and disrupt. A demon thrust a squirming naked man down the devil's throat; the roar of fire drowned his cries. Margery covered her breasts in an attempt to hold herself together; the dark tips ached as invisible fingers pinched them. Another demon helped push in the man's flapping leg with a pitchfork. She felt ter-rified of collision, bloated as a cow's udder, tit pink and squinting.

Jesus sat with his elbows on a table. "I'm not angry with you," he said, "although I allow you to feel pain." Mar-gery felt like she was visiting a childhood home, smaller than remembered. Satan had mauled her for twelve days.

"And I, I—" She shook her head, unable to go on; she sat down and hid her face in her hands. Margery owned little of the world but felt responsible for that portion and more. How strange that the owner of everything felt no responsibility. She was bone weary; the thought rose: How can I get rid of him? He walked away, but slowly. His broad ass was hairless as an egg. She discerned a blindspot behind the clarity of events, an obscurity that jumped and shifted.

44

Jesus perched on the three legged stool in the corner, drinking a glass of wine. His face was softly masculine, almost overdone, eyesockets delicate, nose polished down. He was satisfied with the light falling through the half-open shutters and the wedge of view by now familiar, the neighbor's roof and the hexagonal well. He said mildly, "What will you do now? There can be no more against you but the moon and seven stars. There is scarcely anyone on your side."

"Then we will live together?" There was hatred in her question. Her fading posture and her anger put her in the wrong.

Jesus looked at Margery without recognition and waited long enough for her to feel the thrill of her own absence, as though looking back into a room she'd just stepped out of. He eliminated the particular without granting the absolute. She touched her breasts for comfort. She forgot her intelligence, the beauty of her body, her courage. In forgetting, she lost those qualities. She persisted, "Is there *one* thing about me that you like?" Jesus raised his eyebrows.

She got him aroused, kept him erect, delayed his orgasm. Just in time she let her hand fly off the end of his cock. Still, she knew her energy counted for less because she was not loved. Jesus desired to increase desire by waking and manipulating her points of arousal but they floated in a cosmic dereliction. He tended them insofar as they resembled others of their kind. Margery wanted to be engulfed but retain that loss of self in the memory of her skin. Jesus turned his face away, then allowed her his lips, then yielded his tongue.

Once sex was fully entered nothing was hidden. The skin on her hands tried to memorize a strapping young man planted on his knees waiting to fuck. He was thin from his long calves to his narrow skull yet caressing him was extravagant opulence.

They stood up at the foot of the bed. Margery bent at the waist and Jesus had to crouch. Her toes curled as he guided his cock deep inside her; she dilated and clenched. She saw her legs and those of Jesus—his were squatting and looked rather inexpressive, even comic, turned out as a frog's. He tipped her back and forth with increasing force, thrusting back the borders of their delight; in that motion she was clarified, her giddiness transformed into rapturous calm.

Their flesh emitted fierce oscillations. It seemed odd that they didn't echo in people who surrounded them.

She looked up in surprise. It was 1420; experience was crumbling. A tension rose between the arousal that tried to be everything and the doubt that wouldn't believe it. From her window, Margery saw a civilization that had never entirely come to life. It amazed her that pleasure was so mechanical, so located in space. She had the sinking fear that the party was happening elsewhere. She watched herself convulse from her city's point of view and felt isolated and estranged from her thrill. She wondered if she loved Jesus less. Their little bodies lost significance like words repeated too often. He vaporized as he fucked her, leaving emptiness vibrating in her chest and cunt walls like the blare of a trumpet.

Jesus didn't memorize the serenity of Margery's inner thigh or the jut of her breasts. Perhaps he considered her question, because later he volunteered that he did like something about her: "You have nice ears."

"Too big," Margery said, unbelieving. She looked down at her naked body.

Jesus conceded with a friendly willingness to lose the debate. "The less value you set on yourself, the better."

Margery recognized the arbitrary world. Jesus gazed through her without a flicker of interest. System after system peeled back till there was nothing left but spidery bones. She sank into her grave, crying, "Jesus, don't abandon me! Your angels offer you my tears." She raised her head—a skull that was already empty. He looked at the sockets hopefully. They heard a two-syllabled call followed by the muffled purr of rapidly beating wings.

45

"Hello, Bob," L. says with mild cheer. "What's new and different?" When he speaks, it's not about us but current events, updates—the kind of petty news heads of families xerox and send at Christmas. I listen in disbelief—my aging and death could not go forward without his consent.

My back feels tight. I am aware of the infinity of my longing and my frantic being, and of the relative blankness "outside" where clouds are parsed evenly over the night sky in exasperation. I want a hand to scatter my nipples and cock like dry leaves off my body. I look at the phone which contains his voice. His flesh and blood are sitting by a window—the tops of buildings, a loading dock seven stories down.

It's 2 A.M. his time; I'm in bed in San Francisco. His presence wouldn't cure my loneliness. My life occurs on the heavy satin of his skin yet he won't let me be the cause of stimulation. My egotism is turned upside down. I give him an ultimatum: We've been dating for three years. Let's live together or break up.

L. thinks it over a few months; he has the self-confidence to reject me. I write a blistering letter and show it to my friend Kathy. She advises me to delete the anger and beg: "The only thing I understand is holding you, arousing you, seducing you with tenderness and witnessing your face soften and open, a disheveled openness, your lips swelling, and I am *gazing* into your blue-geode eyes."

"Well," he replies, "I can't say I would necessarily object to seeing each other, but I also wonder how it could be done..."

Margery tried to kiss a leper on the street but he drew back offended. She knelt in a puddle of yellow mud and cried, "Let them lay me naked on a hurdle for all men to wonder at and let them throw slime and spit at me." She was afraid of disease but more terrified of her own unhappiness.

As Jesus withdrew, her flights towards him grew longer; she found a house where leprous women lived. The need to be heard at any cost became a horror of life. One had an ulcer on her breast that ate the surrounding flesh—it fermented and stank like decaying blood. This woman was amazed when Margery pressed her mouth and nose on the festering mess and drank water used to clean it in which flesh had come away.

John was over sixty years old; his hair was silver. He was so drunk that deep in darkness it was bright around him. He leaned against a wall, experiencing its flatness, then the surprising curve of his spine, how he could no longer straighten it. John never asked for much, but to be deprived of his posture seemed like the last straw. He stumbled and laughed, desolate and amused. "I guess it's for the best."

He left his room barefoot and barelegged and his feet coiled in the stairs. John had the sensation of rolling down grassy knolls, slow concussions. He tumbled to the first floor, twisting his head beneath him. Neighbors heard the crash and found him lying alone half dead and streaked with blood.

They said it was Margery's fault because she had moved away to a boarding house. Some said she howled like a dog and ruined her husband. They said if he died she deserved to be hanged. But when Margery and John lived together, people said they broke their vows of chastity; when they went on a pilgrimage, people said they had sex in the forests, groves, and valleys.

John was sewn up and five linen plugs were inserted in the wounds to help them drain. Margery nursed him but after he fell on his head he became self-absorbed, hard to distract; he grew impatient and protested "I'm *thinking,*" as though Margery never used her brain. Should she humor him, demand a reply? He invented memories to lend substance to a mind that sabotaged itself: gifts he had given her, luxurious trips.

A few months later she saw an old man in a shabby black mantle sitting by the road. It was John. He had fainted. She asked if he was sick. "No, no, nothing a doctor can do." He looked downwards, still dazed. "The only healthy people are in the graveyard." Finally he became senile and shit in his linen underwear as he sat by the hearth. The wood was green—water sizzled and steamed out of it. Once she'd had inordinate lust for his body. She worked hard, washing and wringing; it was expensive to keep the fire going all day.

46

All we know of the external world is our own shit, piss, tears, sweat, spit, snot, come, pus, babies, and sometimes blood. Margery said, "For your love I would be chopped up as stew meat for the pot." Her lips parted in sexual hunger. Flesh was not all flesh but partly appetite.

Before she met Jesus, Margery had appeared refined to herself: she was a mayor's daughter. She had recognized in Jesus her own aristocracy. Little by little she adopted vulgar manners to conform to Jesus's view of her; her words retreated to where substances and bodies pass into the world, like this stew-meat image used by the young roofer who rejected her—like the dream of my carcass chopped up in a tub!

I aimed at L. the longing for seduction and credence I had aimed at the world. Naked in bed, he praised my writing—the one thing a stranger could like. He called me and my friends The Writers Who Love Too Much— giddy laughter. Smoothing a wrinkle by my ear, he experimented with my age and aging itself. I felt a surge of hope but the skin sank back to its position.

Margery couldn't catch her breath. Her life was husked away—friends, husband, children, city, house, the temporal order of her community. No one met her with even the smallest portion of her suffering and excitement, no one suspected what she put into her waiting. She felt she was running out of material. All that remained was for Jesus to abandon her. Margery steps into modernity so empty she needs an autobiography.

"Margery, here are some handsome people; they will die before a year is up." Jesus told her when the plague would occur. "I have ordained you to be a mirror and to sorrow." So image and loss are one—an addiction, round and empty in that nothing reflected back but the absence of her own self. She could not materialize.

"Ah, Jesus, you are all generosity."

PART FOUR
Margery's Passion

A-non aperyd verily to hir syght an awngel al clothyd in white beryng an howge boke be-forn hym.

47

Jesus walked towards his Passion with a preoccupied frown. The world grew pale. Mary fell in a dead faint. Jesus lifted her head; she looked up amazed and whispered, "How can I suffer this much sorrow? Let me die before you...never let me suffer this day of sorrow...I can never bear the sorrow I will have from your death. No one can comfort me but you."

Jesus kissed her lips as though she were his little girl. "I will be King, you will be Queen. You will have power over devils—they will be afraid of you, and you never of them. Queen of Heaven, Empress of Hell, and Lady of the World."

Mary could not speak another word so Margery claimed the emotion; she collapsed next to them and caught his ankle, crying, "Kill me rather than abandon me!"

Jesus hissed, "Be still, Margery." His enemies seized him. They dragged him to the ground and pushed him forward so his face hit the pavement and his teeth were dashed together. They spit at him. Jesus smiled foolishly. He took off his own clothes and wrapped his arms around the narrow stone pillar. The freshness of his body could be seen in his skin, milky gold except for some red pimples scattered across his ass.

When the lash struck, he flinched as though it were cold. Something finally happened to his body: the wounds went in one direction and furrowed his skin like patterned cloth. His ribs appeared; he melted like a candle. The switches broke and littered the floor. The spot where he stood filled with blood and he wiped blood from his eyes. He turned to his clothes but his enemies did not give him time to dress. They hurried him along—naked with a rope around his waist. He put his arms in the sleeves and wiped away blood from his face with his tunic. Wherever he stepped he left footprints stained with blood.

Margery and Mary went round on a different path. A white-bearded peasant in a gray surcoat held a plow handle in one hand and goaded a pair of red oxen with his other. He had a wen inside his cheek as big as a pullet's egg. His plowshare turned earth covered by faded winter grass. Margery and Mary could hear the thud of violent blows; they saw Jesus stagger, the cross so heavy he could hardly lift it. They pulled their cloaks over their foreheads like mourning scarfs.

Mary said, "Ah, Jesus ... that heavy cross ..." She fainted, still as the dead. Jesus knelt by Mary to comfort her. Margery fell down too and threw back her head because she couldn't catch her breath. Screams tore her jaws apart, her feeling of constraint dividing over and over as though lavishly blooming.

48

Margery went up to Calvary. Music, soldiers, gambling, silence in the buzzing flies, vendors selling candy and wine. The rocky landscape rose in perspective to a walled hilltop town. A soldier pointed to a tree where Judas hung, intestines spilling from his gaping belly. The Jews tore from Jesus's body a silk cloth that dried blood had glued to his flesh. Jesus saw his dead self and gave up the urge to create relation. His wounds opened and blood ran on every side.

The Jews laid him on the cross. They set a long nail on one palm where the bone was most solid and drove it through with such force it extended far beyond the wood. He was pinned down, mortal. He lost his gold dust, his lips turned blue, his wounds showed purple against chalky skin. All his sinews and veins drew together and his jaw worked in horror. Pain shrank his sinews so his other hand would not reach the hole drilled for it. The Jews fastened ropes to it and pulled. They drew his feet the same way. They crucified his right foot with one nail and over it the left foot with another so that the nerves and veins were extended and broken.

Mary whispered, "Ah, St. Stephen wore a short doublet... black for humility..." She was just a few molecules waked by a breeze.

Margery shoved her aside. *"You accursed Jews, why are you killing Jesus? Kill me instead and let him go!"*

They made a loud shout as they hoisted the cross with Jesus hanging from it a foot or more above the ground and let it drop into the mortise. Jesus shuddered, all his joints burst apart, blood ran down from his wounds. They drove wooden pegs on all sides so the cross would stand firm. The only cloud in the sky hid the sun, making the cloud bright and the sky yellow. Jesus's eyes darkened; he couldn't see except when he expelled blood by squeezing his eyelids. His face grew chalky from loss of blood, his hair and eyes were filled with blood, his ears stopped up with blood.

He tried to stretch himself on the cross to relieve the bitter pain in his arms. The color of death came on, his cheeks hung pale, his ribs could be numbered, his belly collapsed on his back as though he had no stomach, and his nostrils were pinched. His heart was breaking from the pain. He raised his head slightly, inclined to the right. Flies had converged on his face. His pale lips opened and his tongue and teeth were coated with blood.

Terror lifted Margery's amorphous head up through the silence. Her heart thudded slowly. She shrieked in his face, *"Don't abandon me!"* With that Jesus died, his human career ended. His death can't be understood inside the argument of life or the system of Margery's attraction. His hands shrank a little from the nail holes and his feet bore more of his weight. Mary fainted; the sky convulsed in a bruised aqua without moisture and the dry land erupted under their feet. Margery ran in a crouch, ducking bombs and horn blasts from pre-eternity. *Sche cryid, sche roryd & wept sor that many man on hir wonderyd.* Though she expected his death, it was still a shock.

A soldier rode up bearing a lance tipped with iron. The soldier's hair was cropped so close Margery couldn't tell what color it was. When she saw what he intended to do, she picked up a stone and hit the blade from an amazing distance. She kept throwing stones.

The soldier laughed—it was a game to him. He drove his lance into Jesus's side with such force it came out the back. When he withdrew the lance its point was bright red, showing that the heart had been pierced. The soldier's face quickened as a river of dark arterial blood gushed from the wound. The entire scene strobed or flickered, the uncertain light caused by Margery's own eyelids batting. She fell on her knees next to Mary and screamed, *"Cease from your sorrowing—I will sorrow for you!"*

Joseph of Arimathea lowered Jesus's body from the cross and laid it before Mary on a marble slab. The eyes were sunken and full of blood, mouth cold, arms so stiff that the hands could not be raised above the navel. Mary kissed the mouth. Mary Magdalene said, "Let me kiss the feet." Mary's sisters took both hands and kissed them. They clung to Jesus's body, a small raft, but what the infinite means is that we are already in it. Margery ran back and forth; she wanted Jesus for herself; she screamed with awareness till her voice was a pale whistle.

49

Margery was in a state of shock close to wonder; for the moment she knew total freedom. She was ripped in two: half of her was the absent Jesus. It was too soon to bind this injury with strands of language—to make it inevitable, normal. She was just a wound. She fell apart, or opened up.

She lay on her side, rigid, breathing quickly through her nose, making surprised sounds of small hurts. Brittle fear of death replaced endless talk. In Jesus's blank nonrelation she saw her grave, a loss deprived of purpose, unrevealed, unhidden, uninterpreted.

She began the night with her eyes wide open, her senses entirely awake, cold light in the darkness; at dawn she was still focused, wild and cold. Daylight was crisp and weak, celery green. She felt numb; she lost the will to divide inside from outside. She waited for the night and her sorrow to recommence.

She woke at midnight with such heavy grief she was amazed by some deeper Margery who encountered feelings below. She had to wearily reiterate the wooden shutters, her cup on the sill, the stool, the blue covers, the bed. "I can never live through this hour alone"—and then chimes brought the next hour. The air was cold so Margery was cold.

Chimes dragged her unwillingly through the second night. Her muscles hurt. She could not draw into herself enough to sleep. She became the hour of three in the morning, four in the morning. When she journeyed towards the old clock, she was Jesus walking down the corridor and the emptiness stopped assaulting her. She said *hello*, copied his voice like a birdcall: two notes rising, one sinking halfway. She rehearsed the tension in his jaw. His elegant features jumped expressions under the clear sky of his brow.

When information circulates it transforms; she looked from a gold face through strong blue eyes; she walked on long legs with an athlete's pleasure and became the forward stiff-legged gait, the awareness of ass in the short tunic. She abandoned her breasts and belly for a flat expanse of skin. She had lived like a pendulum whose constant travel in space gets it nothing except the loss of a measure of time. She stopped the farcical ticking to establish inaction. The pendulum batted her palms. The terror of the corridor was avoided.

She lurched upright in bed. Her own shout took her by surprise. Her breath was quick, her chest heavy, throat closed off. She tested parts of her body, thinking wild pain must be accompanied by a visible disease or rupture. It amazed her that grief could be pitched so high in a body undefined and slack. She experienced herself most deeply in her love for Jesus. The more she was excluded from that depth, the more she was aware of it. He deprived her of depth without allowing her to be shallow. She tore long welts on her forearms to summon insanity but relentless consciousness was the madness that arrived.

"I've gone crazy," she told herself. "Being mad with grief doesn't mean thrashing around or any activity that puts you in motion or relation. It means lying on your side frozen in one position as hours pass." Margery was grounded. The upward prayer of belief turned back on itself, pinning her to the bed: silence *descends.* The town slept; she heard the rush of water, a torrent pouring through a sluice, and the foggy cry of bitterns from the salt marshes. "It means the story is over." With first light the roosters; with sunrise the dogs.

50

Margery said, "You must comfort yourself and stop sorrowing."

"Ah, where will I go...St. Barbara...hem of blue and silver..." Margery diced carrots and turnips on the trestle table and cooked them in a soup with bread and beer. "Take it away, dear Margery. Give me no food but my own child." Margery saw that Mary's tender smile and courtesy were forms of condescension; Mary's kindness meant to exclude. She comforted Margery but would not allow Margery to comfort her.

A thousand years passed till the third day came. A knock at the door. "It's I, St. Peter, who abandoned Jesus." He fell to his knees, racked with sobs.

Mary consoled him. "Jesus will cheer us up. That child was the best shit I ever had!" Everyone laughed; the hair rose on Margery's neck.

Mary lay in bed sleeping; she smelled like scorched hair. Margery lay beside her, fists clenched against her temples. The hut had no windows; the appalling midday heat stunned her. Mary Magdalene was looking for Jesus at his grave. A blackbird stood with its head to one side listening for worms. Jesus walked stiffly because his flesh had been dead. He stopped behind her. "Why are you crying?"

Mary Magdalene jumped and spun around; she did not recognize Jesus dressed like a gardener in a jerkin and straw hat. He said, "Mary." His voice was full of dirt, gritty. She felt her eyeballs swell in her head. She bent to kiss his feet but Jesus rasped, "Don't touch me."

Mary Magdalene looked miserable. Margery thought if Jesus cried *Touch me not* to her, she would crumble along with the rest of her meager story.

51

Margery, Mary, Peter, Thomas, and Mary's sisters all stood up when Jesus stepped into the sweltering bunker. He shuffled woodenly and brought into the terrible shack a flat stench. He said in the gravelly whisper of the undead, "Hello, mother."

The skin prickled on Thomas's back; he guarded his throat in an instinctive gesture. Jesus grabbed Thomas's fingers and jammed them into the wound in his chest with a look of rapture. Jesus gritted his teeth like L. does during orgasm, desiring sensation but unwilling to be moved by it. Peter gaped in horror at the risen dead and met its enthusiasm with revulsion. Margery fell backwards onto her chair. She thought her cries were drowned by organ music. Others remember Margery as a frenetic dog.

Jesus said, "Will someone put her out?" She smelled the wounds, the shredded hands.

Mary said, *"Art yu my swete Sone, Ihesu?"*

"I am your son." He lifted and kissed her. Mary searched his body as though she had lost her place. She took his hand and pressed it to her lips. Her cheek retained his blood and a dangling ribbon of flesh. Mary's eyes glinted with sardonic humor which she shared with Jesus— their eyebrows raised in amusement—as she turned her gory face for everyone to see.

Margery was entirely gazing, so terrified she didn't swallow her spit. She became aware that she was stranded in a remote desert in a stifling concrete bunker. Its tin roof cracked in the heat. She felt the weight of the arbitrary setting: an unlimited desert came into view, entered without clothes or memory. Her vision began to strobe; Mary and Jesus crackled with beams of winter light raying out sovereignty, casting faint shadows. Then they were shabby derelicts, one in grimy blue rags, the other in a stiff shroud reeking of decaying blood.

52

"All my pain is gone. Mother, ask me anything." Jesus answered her questions.

Margery rose to embrace Jesus but he raised his arm against her, his palm flat as a door. Her desire for conclusion was intensely gratified. You could say Jesus created her in that instant: through him she glimpsed a Margery too abandoned to imagine on her own. Stiff with panic, she threw out her arms hopelessly as though warding off a wrecking ball. Her chest felt sore and heavy. Margery had not understood the stakes in the first place—she would rot in the dirt.

She didn't doubt there *were* saints in heaven who had never seen the terrible expression Jesus wore: coldly sympathetic. Each saint touched one version of Jesus; hers was a charming reserved brown-haired blond with bone-tipped shoulders, brilliant skin whose chest hairs could be counted, tiny pink nipples, tiny navel, broad hips, and long blond legs.

Mary brought Margery a bowl of her own soup. Margery set the spoon down. Jesus tried to comfort her too. He felt newly tender now that the issue of eternity was behind them. Her life broke into withering ironies. "Do you want to meet in a half hour?" Jesus asked mildly, with a clarity that sees pain as decoration.

When they met, he said, "Your blue eyes are beautiful." He felt their relationship was her creation. Still, he reminded her of adventures they'd had together in Italy, as though looking through photos and inviting her to share a tremulous nostalgia: he added gold to the highlights on folds of mountain and cloth. Every image was a farewell to what it portrayed. He retained the pleasant stories and left the cruel ones to her.

He didn't look at her. "Well, Margery…" His eyes crumpled and his lips gave way. His head dropped a few inches and he began to cry a little. Jesus reduced Margery's bid for transcendence to a scrapbook of *experiences*. Her eyes remained dry; she'd already given her tears away. She asked to see more of him but he said he was too busy, as though he had to work.

The gods weren't counting on Margery; they offered no strong belief in the value of life. Their lack of faith made her doubt herself from childhood to that instant. It was no use going back to yesterday since she had been a different person then.

Jesus discarded her dumb love and abandoned her. From there, Margery might have advanced to real faith— a vocation *begun in tears*, cracked open as she was, left for dead as she was. I don't know what that faith would be. Margery did not accept this emptiness; instead, she dilated on the point of rejection.

53

Margery woke before dawn when she had nothing. She pulled a blanket over her body as though she were sick but she was also the disease, a noxious failure she wanted to hide. She covered her eyes from shame. She had been abandoned forever, a verdict passed for the first time each second. She couldn't speak. During the day her surroundings and companions joined in her broad prosaic failure but the fact of rejection startled her as though she were falling down a stairway.

Anxious desolation of the day became anxious desire at night. She had come to a halt but her being was still hurtling. Her membranes rang with anticipation. Her muscles twitched and tugged and when she came her body slowly curled towards the hateful excitement like paper towards a flame. The soft explosions could not consume the tenderness she felt for Jesus. She had made an impossible wish. Now she had nothing but vehement desire that was so exasperated she turned her face and threw out her hands as though to a witness.

Because she desired Jesus she didn't realize that in their separation he got what he wanted. Her cunt dripped like the shinbone of a saint that weeps in continuous relation to God. Her hips rolled, her nipples hardened, her tissues hurt with pleasure. Her body was still his lover. Ecstasies boiled up and popped just under her skin in steady bursts, the physical evidence of destitution. She rubbed herself wearily. What gesture indicates the desire for more life? When she heard a creak, she thought it was his foot on the tread.

His voice, a clarinet; his eyes, blue geodes; the tilt of his head; the hair tumbling down his brow; his dazzled expression; his small translucent teeth; his pointed tongue; his straight back; the vein running down his inner thigh; the ankle and the arch. He is already breaking into parts. More than that: Margery's urge to strip Jesus, to complete him, to uncover, to make him respond and respond. There *is* no body that precedes his body yet it is overwhelmingly passive. Panicked, she looks for it in continual expectation of making love. She *separates* his knees, *opens* his crotch; her hand on his hip *rotates* his torso; she *shoves* his knees to his ears, his asshole contracts, the amazing flesh moves as the floor slides out from under her. She *tips* his head back, *exposes* his throat. Trying to explain him she dismantles a complex of refinements—ropy strands of sperm—there won't be any Jesus after Margery outdoes the cross.

The mirror sickened her. Her features hung from a billowing curtain; her hair was gray, thin, her lips had thinned, and her mouth pulled downwards, stale and dishonest. Injustice without remedy. The skin on her hands and face had gleamed with indestructible youth but Jesus withdrew the body's beauty.

In her descent each basement gave way to a deeper one. How do we bear the loss of opportunity and life? She recoiled with crisp fear from elderly friends: they dragged her into the grave. She turned away from young people; their tight juicy skin was a brutal assault, was a darkness, future as past. Friends spasmed with pleasure as their bodies faltered, saw the last light as they sifted into dust. Death weakened Margery because she no longer held a belief that could survive its spotlight—neither do I.

Towards the end of the night, Margery climbed in with John. He propped his head on his elbow and gazed at her; he didn't exactly know her but she couldn't cry until she'd felt some warmth. John dangled his fingers over hers and rubbed his rather thick pinky nail against the tip of her thumb as his father used to do for hours when John lay in his crib. The torrent flowed and John whimpered in sympathetic desolation, everything concentrated in the friction of nail on skin. He thought it was his own sorrow and his caresses were aware, his heart blinking in the early dawn. His affection was comforting and hard to bear. Insidiously, the old pleasure fanned out like wings until the fact of rejection startled her with a sickening shift and a jolt of adrenaline dried her tears.

Everything she knew was against her. Her perilous journeys had been conversations with Jesus. There were sea captains to guide her and bishops to vanquish like small dragons. Death had become a task to perform, an achievement. The problem was stupid: How do you find your way in empty desert when you have become that desert? She wanted to shed the knowledge of life and death now that such knowledge could not lead outside itself, could not be used to improve her position. Margery fell back with a feeling of vertigo. She looked at her open fingers.

54

Margery rolled on her back; she lay musing, suddenly very comfortable, laughing, imagining long conversations and the weight of his head on her shoulder. She straightened her legs—a moment of relief. All day near and distant shutters banged open and closed; she heard the flat-footed voice of a child. She wanted to amuse Jesus and to describe her nights. His withdrawal was a story, like all her stories, for him.

She kindled hope so she could love unimpeded for another hour. Moist air blurred the moon's edge. He's testing her—because rejection is the sentiment of the era. She imagined reconciliations; they had happened before. He's not sure how to approach her—Margery, is it too late for us to start again?

She saw him talking through a steady smile, eyes lowered, lashes' gold dust, features painful with meaning. She held her arms out in the intensity of contradiction. "You couldn't *stand* the intimacy we shared if you didn't love me. I am always aroused, which proves my point."

She had become a contradiction so she stated it with hectic energy to save herself, as though Jesus would have to return once it was clearly put: "Your ability to change my life, your unwillingness to do so."

What quality did she love in Jesus? "An elegant loneliness which I desire."

Margery wakes before dawn so furious that Jesus is a bitter taste in her mouth. Under a strange sky, in the middle of nowhere, only her fury is familiar. She wants to hurl her life at him like a bomb. She has to number her grievances as she lies rigid in the dark, knocking her feet together. She finally calls him a prick, reluctantly losing grandeur and scale. Jesus pretends to die, then lets her die for real. She mentally shouts *Get away!* as though he's attacking.

Light pushes through, wan and gray; for an hour bird chatter dominates the city. She tries to protect herself by attacking him. She abandons Jesus.

"Your hips are too wide, you are knock-kneed. Your nipples are too small, you have pimples on your ass." She drags farts out of him, his ignorant seagull expression as people look up and sniff and her insides roll with joy. She doesn't know how to diminish him. "He's just a *boy*, but *extremely beautiful*," she adds, puzzled. She could never deface that beauty but she pulls his soul apart like tissue.

She tries again to steady and enclose the catastrophe. A boy, a charming boy who is tender, cruel, who treats me any way he likes. Who never endorses me, whose rapture breaks with everything, moments of innocence and intoxication, who arrives with gifts...

In her bed she sees them from above. Jesus strides too fast down the gray muddy road, his beauty, his clothes, her crude white gown, her clumsy gestures, questions. She follows like a servant (he relates to servants). She looks dwarfish, the huge white clown head, the frowning clown's farce of self-advancement.

"You will never know anything till you have to work for a living. You bought me clothes and took me to Italy—you never gave me a penny of real support."

In her mind her voice rings but Jesus's half-smile challenges these facts by not responding to them. She can't wound him anymore than she could heal him—a block of wood failed to become a boy. Her grievances are old and feeble in their infancy. At whatever level she rejects him, she sees that her love exists *below* that level. She can't get to a bedrock beneath her love or to a Margery that hasn't already been abandoned. Jesus will not be transformed by Margery's anger. She throws up an arm to ward him off. *"Get away from me!"*—as though he assaults her in a nightmare.

55

The sun rose, house wrens sang below the eaves, dogs barked. I describe Margery's suffering as though it lasted a few days instead of years. We are in the middle of our lives and we are breaking down. Although I think only of L., my senses jump when I see his image, name, or handwriting as though something is about to happen. What remains?

Through the window, only a few feet away, a rat perched on a decayed fence; its fur was the same gray as the weathered cedar. It drew its legs under its body like a sphinx; its beady eyes wore the peace of authority at the top of a long mule face. Her desire for transcendence was leaching into nostalgia for the view, her cup, the blue covers.

There was a haze or mist, the sky seemed sooty a long way off—farmers burning land? Margery recoiled from the voice in her head as it talked to her. No use trying to be two people, she thought. She was lonely for company and longed to be even in the hearing of other voices.

She had no happiness or faith as complete as her rich, obsessive grief. Reluctantly she abandoned grief and later its repetitions droning on and on, so arid that language was exhausted. Without Jesus, Margery's story was open ended. She began to accept interim life and the lie of the partial truth.

Jesus returned twice to Margery. He gave her ten pounds towards her support, a large sum at that time, which she was glad to have.

Later he said, "I always felt guilty about desiring other people. If that was my negation of you, was the fault mine? My ambivalence and your demands were part of the erotics of our relationship. I didn't always treat you well—I never tried to hurt you." But Jesus couldn't do or say anything to alter the figure always turning away in her imagination.

56

A flock of angels wear the wide eyes of departure; their gold hair is longer and curlier than strictly fashionable. Their wings open in a trance: powder blue fading to black banded in chestnut, the plumage believable the more unbelievable it looks.

A woman famous for her tears turned a corner in the 1430s and wrote the story of her life. I respond to the failure that permeates her book: Margery lacked a criterion for the discernment of spirits.

She didn't lack faith in prayer or anecdote. She took for granted the belief that a pear has flavor, all the ecstasy of description. The angels have full lips; their features are soft but their heavy necks seem masculine. I have less faith in existence than Margery so I describe it more thoroughly.

Margery tried to change her future by recasting herself in the medium where she was strong. Her book opens an argument so final judgment can't be passed; it rebuilds the exterior that love had erected, purveys an endless continuity, recreates the promise of life-as-it-is.

She turned her second-rate obsession into her last bid for endless response, a self asserted just as the world withdrew its support. She fell for so long she lost the sensation. Margery still loved the strength of words but she had no world to use them on. Let Jesus float forever, a wicked god condemned to her shifting currents of language that leave him dependent. She acknowledged an interrupted feeling, belief withdrew and entered on a higher level as doubt.

Margery sees she is abandoned, that she will age and die alone, but only in a story. When her character knows that, what does it know? Emptiness is *contained* in the work. She's writing in the early morning. Suddenly she's aware of her body, its being underneath her, heavy and contorted. Her left leg crosses over the right, toes press against the floor for stability. Her neck aches. Her cunt is minimal. The skin on the back of her hands is thin and dry. Her hair hangs in her eyes and her mouth tastes like rust. But to note all this is to track her awareness shifting through a remote terrain.

A hornet hovers next to the windowpane, bouncing against it. That's Jesus trying to get in, Margery tells herself without conviction. She's comfortable for the moment—for the moment that lives and dies.

She had access to the body of Jesus—that is, belief in the value of life and such ecstasy as my corruptible tongue cannot express. I reconstruct the memory of that access as a ruin, a hollow space inside meaning, a vehicle for travel. Still, Jesus can lift me out of time to be his lover.

I leave Margery in a suspended moment as the inevitability of L. subsides along with my fear of dying. I dreamt that Margery wants to see me. Who would know to pass himself off as her? Only L., I surmise, because I asked him not to contact me. Now *I* am the god of nonrelation. If he takes my place as Margery, do I take his place as

Jesus? At last my position is not so fixed. I feel the anguish of rejecting him, but I'm not sure I do—a quandary of wanting and not wanting.

A failed saint turns to autobiography. Love *amazes* me; I *exult* in my luck, in our sex; L. *exasperates* me; I am *exasperating*; I am *abandoned*. I want to contain my rambling story in a few words.

exult, exasperate, abandon, amaze

MY MARGERY, MARGERY'S BOB

Margery Kempe is a novel of obsession, grief, and farce, loss of self and excess of self. The unrequitedness of life in general is conveyed through the specifics of a love story. A woman who lived in the first part of the fifteenth century tries and fails to become a saint. Her steamy romance with Jesus is framed by Bob's obsessive love for a young man, L., until the two stories merge to become one: "Bob" becomes Margery, L. becomes Jesus. Bob's ability to enter the fifteenth century is "underwritten" by Margery's own travel through time to the events of Jesus' life.

I did not want *Margery* to be an historical novel, a genre that hardly interests me (unless executed by Flaubert and a few others). What is an historical novel? A time machine that seems to restore another era and give us access to its citizens. That is, we get to know Alexander the Great. There's a lie involved, but is that lie different from the lie fiction generally tells? An historical novel describes people and events we are already loyal to because they occur in the world we inhabit, yet they are unapproachable for that very reason. Alexander the Great will always be unknowable, his story beyond my control.

I wanted to use Margery's story, but also to let it alone, to retain the Margery who coextends—however distantly—

with the world the reader inhabits. What drew me to Margery's life could only be known by us in the present: the difference between her high aspiration and her failure. In a way, my book is about what Margery could not know about herself—the mix of periods her story embodies (medieval, modern). I feel this describes my own condition—a mix of periods in which scales of judgment, of interpretation, do not jibe. Will the future understand this disparity?

How to use historical matter and be true? True to what? Over the course of five years I grappled with this question. I had to import a version of integrity into the genre. How do you not lie in fiction? Some modernist (and premodern!) answers: to "bare the device"; to assert the reader's present time (the time of the reading, art as object); to challenge linear time; to expose the writer's point of view; to meld figure and ground. Then how to use historical matter? I pressured the genre by bringing my relation to this slice of history into the book. History is endlessly porous; so instead of creating a middle distance, I used extreme close-ups, historical long shots, and autobiography.

My books usually contain an element of collaboration; in this case I asked about forty friends for observations and memories about their bodies. Those intimate details are applied to—that is, stitched into—remote fifteenth-century characters. Interior life is clearly attributed—in the acknowledgements! Some of these observations have been published by their authors. They are not descriptions of fictional characters in the usual sense, but random pleasures and fears that couldn't possibly be known from the middle distance. They atomize interior life, pressure the idea of historical re-creation (locating Ed's fear of death inside the Vicar of St. Stephen) and at the same time they summon a community (of friends, of physical anarchy) in which to stage my obsession. Physical life, obsession: history as disjunction, a gap.

I created an aesthetic relationship with history by setting limits. I refrained from reading a book about Margery till I was done with the novel, confining myself to her self-description. I limited descriptions to certain aspects of fifteenth-century life, especially clothes, food, and physical gestures. I did not read conventional histories to "fill in." Instead, I married my prose to Margery's, confecting a sentence halfway between us, feeling Margery and the period through the rhythm of her language (another kind of collaboration). Most of the texts I used were books of hours, saints' lives and such from the fourteenth and fifteenth centuries, following the model of Tzvetan Todorov's beautiful *Conquest of America*, a reading of many texts from the period.

I am interested in the puzzle of using real people in fiction; my fictions have been autobiographies. I suppose I have staged Margery's story in the theater of autobiography, building aesthetics out of the interpenetration of fact and fiction. For me, the world of fact is made up of fiction, from "ideological state apparatuses," to the sale of lifestyle, to the all-and-nothing of language itself. And, of course, the world of fiction is a fact.

Is autobiography a subset of history? I'm an autobiographer, and Kempe, the failed saint, wrote the first autobiography in English (in about 1430). This is only one of the parallels I make to give the historical matter a vector. I draw together the emergence of the modern self and the end of the modern self, the decaying society in which Kempe lived, the decaying society in which I live, and our respective plagues. L.'s ruling-class status equals the divinity of Jesus. (In the fifteenth century, gods were closer to mortals—about as close as a Rockefeller.) The two stories are like transparencies; each can be read only in terms of the other.

The present extends in all directions; it orders the future

and reorders the past. Margery's story can be taken as one huge metaphor to describe Bob's state of mind. That is, as the second term of a metaphor that describes the present.

But writing about a historical subject does not mean writing from the other side of history. That's what makes me uneasy about the fashion for movies and books that seem to "restore" a period as one would restore a house—a distasteful tourism masquerading as good taste. Antique restoration is a postmodern mode, from *Masterpiece Theater* to the many fundamentalisms in this country and abroad. It is a postmodern desire to want a city or even a parlor to be an exact duplication of an earlier period. These fundamentalisms all speak to the yearning to be authentic, to be part of a recognizable order.

Instead, I feel I am a contributor to Margery's life, an event in her posthumous life, and she has certainly contributed to my own sense of myself. Our lives are intertwined. Her posthumous life's twists and turns allow me to adopt that line of thought. Margery did me the favor of disappearing for four centuries. She was all but forgotten except for a few lovely prayers. She is a twentieth-century phenomenon. Her book was discovered in the library of Col. Butler-Bowdon's sixteenth-century manor house and published in 1934. Margery wakes up in this century as though she experienced a wonderfully prolonged coming out in which the necessity to tell her story prevailed. But Butler-Bowdon, her Prince Charming, referred to her in his preface as "poor Margery." She was disappointing—her vulgarity, self-aggrandizement, and the faults in her piety. The distinct phases of her reputation duplicate other coming outs: first the establishment was ashamed of her because she was a noisy woman and inadequate saint; then feminism glorified her strength; and now the great maw of cultural studies absorbs her life, which becomes one more example in the history of subjectivity and daily life.

"Queering" the past (as the MLA puts it) is hardly an issue for me: What else can I do? Margery prostrated herself "with inordinate lust" before the "members" of world religions—I can do no less. I am more attracted to dubious moments of explosion and disjunction than, say, to the life of Michelangelo, the world-historical genius who defines his period. *Margery* is a queer version of disintegration that includes (takes with it) a central myth of our culture. Perhaps I am as angry as Cousin Bette, and perhaps anger is a defining position. I don't mind a reaction of shock—there's plenty of aggression in the book. Shock, confusion, sexual arousal—all acceptable.

The actual forms we take are a kind of extremity we are driven to in a quest for love. We exist to desire and be desired. Or, more roundly, we make ourselves "different" and "same" in order to be loved (if only by the world). And behind this is the mystery of form, how weird and even unendurable it is to be one thing (race, sexuality, gender) rather than another.

When I become Margery, I can no more "control" the import of my literary drag than I could if I dressed as a woman, pursuing an inner necessity whose explanations and effects would be contradictory at best. But maybe that impurity, which is an expression of a problem rather than a way of containing or explaining it, is the way I handle the ever-crossing circuits of narration.

To make an object of the book, to suppress figure and ground, I developed a kind of minimalism amid the excess. I piled up declarative sentences. I used birds and bird calls every few pages. I researched where a certain bird would visit during a given season, say, "the whickering trill of a grebe" in Margery's vision of the Holy Land during December, 0000, the year of Jesus' birth. And I hung the novel on four words—*exalt*, *exasperate*, *abandon*, *amaze*—that appear again and again, a reduced version of the whole book.

Margery is a tale of middle-aged breakdown (those other middle ages) for Margery and Bob equally. By the end of the book, both accept the partial truth of life in the moment—including an acceptance of death, which in the logic of the book means the reduction of the fear of death, and so the end of obsession. Still, Bob and Margery persist in wanting to be lifted out of history and see their books as another stab at rewriting the end.

—ROBERT GLÜCK
2000

OTHER NEW YORK REVIEW CLASSICS

For a complete list of titles, visit www.nyrb.com or write to:
Catalog Requests, NYRB, 435 Hudson Street, New York, NY 10014